# If it doesn't kill you

by Margaret Bechard

VIKING

For Alex, Nick, and Peter. And Ian, too.
Thanks for all the stories.

VIKING
Published by the Penguin Group
Penguin Putnam Books for Young Readers,
345 Hudson Street, New York, New York 10014, U.S.A.
Penguin Books Ltd, 27 Wrights Lane, London W8 5TZ, England
Penguin Books Australia Ltd, Ringwood, Victoria, Australia
Penguin Books Canada Ltd, 10 Alcorn Avenue, Toronto, Ontario, Canada M4V 3B2
Penguin Books (N.Z.) Ltd, 182–190 Wairau Road, Auckland 10, New Zealand

Penguin Books Ltd, Registered Offices: Harmondsworth, Middlesex, England

First published in 1999 by Viking,
a member of Penguin Putnam Books for Young Readers.

1  3  5  7  9  10  8  6  4  2

Copyright © Margaret Bechard, 1999
All rights reserved

LIBRARY OF CONGRESS CATALOGING-IN-PUBLICATION DATA
Bechard, Margaret.
If it doesn't kill you / Margaret Bechard.  p. cm.
Summary: High school freshman Ben should be enjoying playing
football, meeting girls, and going to parties, but he's too busy
trying to cope with his father's moving out to live with another man.
ISBN 0-670-88547-9
[1. Homosexuality—Fiction. 2. Fathers and sons—Fiction.
3. High schools—Fiction. 4. Schools—Fiction. 5. Interpersonal
relations—Fiction.]  I. Title.
PZ7.B38066If 1999 [Fic]—dc21 98-49553 CIP AC

Printed in U.S.A.
Set in Plantin

## Also by Margaret Bechard

*My Mom Married the Principal*
*Star Hatchling*
*Really No Big Deal*
*Tory and Me and the Spirit of True Love*
*My Sister, My Science Report*

# Chapter One

I can hear the shouts and laughter from the locker room behind me. Sergio swearing at Ty for stealing his socks. Jason trying to sing a Beastie Boys song. I hate being one of the first guys out.

I wait at the big double doors, looking out the little window. Clumps of parents are scattered around the sidewalk. I scan the parking lot, but there's no sign of Mom's car. I rub my shoulder. I'm going to have a bruise from when I blocked that big-ass Number 32 on the Beaverton line. But he never knew what hit him. I grin and push open the door and step outside.

The cold November air feels good after the hot, stale air of the locker room. Smells a lot better, too. I suck in a big, deep breath.

Mr. Yamaguchi spots me and walks over. "Good game, Ben!"

"Thanks."

Chris bangs through the door behind us. "We lost, Dad. The game sucked."

"Well, Beaverton's a tough team. But Ben here had some great plays. That was some fine football."

I hate it when parents do this stuff, especially when their own kid is standing right there. I look at Chris, and he shrugs. "I'm just good at knocking guys down, I guess," I say, and Mr. Yamaguchi laughs like this is really hilarious.

"Is it true we're the worst freshman team in the history of the school?" Chris asks.

I don't know a lot of the guys on the team real well. We almost all went to different middle schools. But just about everybody thinks I'm some kind of walking history book of Willamette View football. "I dunno," I say.

"Believe me," Mr. Yamaguchi says. "You're not the worst team in the history of *this* school." He gives me a funny little half smile. "I played football here with your dad, you know. When your grandpa was coach. Back in the Ice Age."

Chris groans, but I really look at Mr. Yamaguchi for the first time. "You played football?"

He laughs and pats his fat stomach. "Hard to believe now. I mostly kept the bench warm for the other guys, but I had my moments." He laughs again. "Not like your dad, of course. Or you, out there today. I think you've got your dad's hands."

I look down at my sneakers. I don't know what I'm supposed to say.

"Too bad your dad can't come watch you play. I guess he works afternoons?"

"Yeah." I really do not want to talk about Dad. I give Chris a shove with my gear bag. "At least that was our last game. At least the season's over."

"2–7," Chris says. "I don't know how we managed to win two."

"2–7 is nothing to be ashamed of," Mr. Yamaguchi says. He puts a hand on my shoulder, the other on Chris's. "And there's always next year. And the year after. You guys have a lot of football ahead of you."

It sounds like a threat to me, but I don't say anything.

"You need a ride home tonight, Ben?" Mr. Yamaguchi asks.

"No. My mom's picking me up."

"Okay then." He slaps my arm. "Good game," he says again.

"You going to the varsity game tonight?" Chris asks me. It's the last game of the regular season, before the play-offs start. Our varsity team will play Beaverton's tonight. Beaverton's varsity sucks. "I don't know, man," I say. "I think I have stuff to do at home." I really don't feel like watching our varsity win again.

"See you Monday then," Chris says, and he and his dad cross the wet parking lot to their Voyager.

The Beaverton bus pulls out with a loud screech, in a cloud of diesel. You can hear their team shouting and cheering. The rest of the Willamette View team trickles out of the locker room. We all say "Good game" to each other. Mrs. Orton, my Spanish teacher, stops and gives me a hug. Her son plays tight end. She comes to all the games. "What a heartbreaker, Ben," she says. She has a Southern accent, and it makes her sound really sad.

The parking lot is pretty empty. Not a lot of people come to the freshman football games. A few parents. Sean

3

Kotowolski's girlfriend and some buddies of hers. I watch the last couple of cars pull out, mostly dads driving.

I look down at my hands. I definitely don't have Dad's hands. I'm sort of clumsy with the ball. Grandpa always said Dad had solid hands. Dad had speed and agility. I have size and strength. I have power.

Now that I've gotten started, I just keep going. I start listing all the ways I'm totally different from my dad. I've done this a lot since he moved out last May, and I'm really good at it. I have blond hair, his hair is brown. I have blue eyes, his are much more green. He was a quarterback. I'm a fullback and a defensive end.

Before he moved out, back last May, Dad said, "Believe me, Ben. This is the hardest thing I've ever had to do. But I just can't live here anymore."

I close my eyes for a second. Get my concentration back. He never even played freshman football. He went straight to varsity. I'm good at math. I suck at English and writing and crap like that. I'm taking Spanish, not French. I think *Aliens* is a way better movie than *Alien*.

By the time Mom shows up, my list is long, and it's starting to drizzle.

"Sorry, sorry, sorry," she says as she moves to the passenger seat and fastens her seat belt. "The freeway was bumper to bumper."

"It's okay," I say. I toss my gear in the back of the Volvo and climb into the driver's seat. "You're not that late." I fasten my seat belt, let off the emergency brake, and put the car in drive.

"Go slow now. Turn on your headlights, it's getting dark. And it's been raining. The roads might be slick."

"I know, Mom." She's sitting up real straight, her fingers pressing into the dashboard. "I've been driving for two months now. You can probably start to relax."

"I am relaxed. Watch for cars when you pull out. Turn on your signal."

For just a second, I think about gunning it out of the parking lot. Zero to sixty. Give her something to really get tense about. But I don't. I wait for the oncoming cars and then pull out, slowly.

"Watch this UPS truck now! How was the game?"

"I see the truck, Mom. We lost."

"Oh, sweetie." Her eyes flicker to me, then snap back to the road. "How bad?"

"35–14."

She sucks in her breath and winces. "Ouch. How did *you* do?"

I ease into the left turn lane. Slow to a stop to wait for the green light. "Okay. We held them scoreless for the fourth quarter. And I had two interceptions."

She grins. "Good for you. Turn on your wipers. Watch this old man. Let him cross first."

I manage to get us all the way to our street without hitting any trucks or cars or little old men.

"Is your bag full of muddy stuff?" Mom asks.

"Yeah." I turn into our cul-de-sac. "I have to get the jersey washed and have it back next week."

We both see the cat at the same time, a black-and-white blur dashing out from under the hedge in front of the Lowerys' old house.

"Look out!" Mom shrieks.

I fumble my foot off the gas, bang it against the brake. I

5

finally manage to get on top of the brake pedal and stomp it as hard as I can. The Volvo rocks to a stop.

We sit there for a second, neither one of us saying anything. I'm glad the seat belt tightened. I figure it's the only thing keeping my heart inside my chest. "Did I hit it?"

"I don't know." She peels her fingers off the dashboard and looks out her window. "I don't see it." She looks back at me. "I didn't feel a thump. Did you feel a thump?"

I shut my eyes. I really don't want to think about this. I shake my head.

She sighs. "Well, I suppose you'd better check."

I open my eyes. "Check for what?"

"For the cat, Ben. As a driver, you have to accept certain responsibilities. . . ."

"Okay, okay." I climb out of the car and stand there, looking up and down the street. I'm thinking maybe I'll see the stupid cat sitting there under the hedge, giving me a dirty look. But there's no cat.

I bend down and look underneath the car. It's dark, and it smells faintly of oil and mud. I don't see anything, and I think, good, we missed it. But then I see a shadowy lump near the back tire.

I stand up. "I think I see it," I say to Mom through the window.

She makes a face. "Great. Is it dead?"

"I can't tell."

"Well, see if it's . . . okay."

I sigh. If it's alive, what are we going to do? Give it CPR? Call 911? "I'm not going to touch it," I say.

"No, no. Don't *touch* it."

I go to the back and crouch down. It's the cat, all right.

Its white fur is splotched with black patches. In the street-light, I can't tell if they're blood or grease or just regular cat spots. I can't tell if it's dead or alive.

I stand up, and something hits me, hard, in the middle of the back. I turn around. It's a girl. She hits me again, in the chest. With her fist.

"Cat murderer!" she screams.

I can see Mom, twisting around in the front seat, her mouth a round O of surprise.

"Cat murderer!" the girl shouts again.

I want to say that it was an accident. I want to say that I've only been driving for a couple of months, that it was my first emergency braking situation. But instead I say, "Maybe it's just wounded."

"Wounded? You don't get wounded by a car, you moron." And she kneels down on the wet pavement, reaches under the car, and pulls the cat out.

You're not supposed to move people who've been injured in car accidents. They say that all the time on *Real Stories of Paramedics*. Only I don't know about cats. And I don't want her to call me a moron again. So I don't say anything.

She straightens up with the cat cradled in her arms. It's very limp, but I think it's breathing. The girl has a lot of long, black hair. Kind of frizzy Chelsea Clinton hair. Only she's cuter than Chelsea Clinton. And younger. Probably about my age. And I'm wondering what she thinks about me. If she might think I'm okay-looking.

She looks up at me. "Stupid moron," she says. And she turns and walks up the driveway and into the Lowerys' old house.

Mom has gotten out of the car. She's standing on the

other side, looking over the roof at the house. "There was a U-Haul there this morning. They must have just moved in today. It'll be nice to have some new neighbors." She looks at me. "Maybe I'll bring over a plate of cookies some time."

"Sure." Welcome to the neighborhood. Here's some cookies. Sorry about the cat. We both climb back into the car, and I drive, very slowly and very carefully, across the street and into our garage.

The message light on the phone is flashing. Two messages.

The first one is Grandma. "Oh. I hate these machines. You just call me back."

Grandma is Dad's mom. "What do you suppose she wants?" I ask.

Mom sighs. "I have no idea."

The tape clicks, spins, advances to the next message. It's Dad. "Hey, Ben. Just thought I'd give you a call." He pauses, and in the background, I can hear people talking. Guys talking. One of them is probably Keith. I don't look at Mom, and I know she's not looking at me. "Well. When you get a chance, give me a call back." He hangs up.

I push the erase button. "I'm not calling him back."

"That's fine," Mom says. She reaches out like she's going to pat my head or something, then drops her hand. "Look. I've got to go back out tonight. There's this client dinner thing." She makes a face. She started working full-time in June. Now it seems like she works all the time. "I'll leave you some money to order a pizza, okay?"

"Sure."

"You could ask somebody over, you know. How about Jeremy?"

8

Jeremy Matson and I were pretty good friends, back in elementary school and middle school. But I haven't seen much of him since high school started. We only have one class together. And he's in band. He's always hanging out with the band nerds, and I hang out with the freshman jocks. It's way too much to explain to Mom. "No. That's okay."

She sighs and goes down the hall to her room.

She leaves about an hour later, and I'm sort of glad when she's gone. I like having the house to myself.

I order the pizza, then I grab a diet Coke and take it into the living room. I drink half the Coke, fast, and burp loudly. I stand there, in the dark, looking out at the Lowerys' house. The cat girl's house.

Two cars pull up. A woman gets out of the silver Honda. A man gets out of the Trooper. The man puts his arm around the woman, and she says something, and he laughs. They walk up the steps together. It's like watching TV with the mute on. A commercial for greeting cards maybe. Or long-distance phone service. I half expect the cat girl to coming running out, all of them hugging on the porch. But she doesn't. The two adults just disappear inside.

"I just can't go on living a lie anymore, Ben." That's what Dad said, back in May. "I can't go on pretending. It's not fair to me or to you or to your mother."

I go back into the family room. I click on the TV and surf through the channels. There's not a lot on on Friday night. Stupid sitcoms and newsmagazine shows. There's a James Bond movie on HBO. Dad hates these new movies. He says Sean Connery is absolutely the only real James Bond. Which is total bull. I grab another Coke and sit down to watch.

# Chapter Two

I don't see the cat girl again on Saturday or Sunday. And even though Mom wants me to, I don't drive again, either. I keep thinking about that stupid cat. I wonder if it goes on your permanent driving record. Running over a cat.

When I get to school on Monday morning, they've finally taken down the pumpkins and scarecrows and the ads for the Halloween dance. Instead, there's a big paper banner stretched across the front of the commons. "We ♥ Freshman Football!" It has all our names written along the sides in fluorescent paint and glitter.

They've spelled my name wrong.

"Gear-*heart*." Jeremy comes up behind me. He swings his clarinet case toward the sign. "I kind of like it. It sounds like RoboCop's sidekick."

I shake my head. "How come they can spell Yamaguchi right. And Kotowolski?"

"The Leadership Class did it, Ben," Jeremy says. "What do you expect? That's a pretty good wolverine, though. Do you know who drew it?"

I shake my head. They can draw great wolverines, but they can't spell Gearhart?

There's a sign on my locker. It's shaped like a jersey, with my number on it, and it says, "Good job, Ben." I pull it off. As I'm closing my locker, two of the JV cheerleaders, Mandy and Kirsten, bounce up.

"We're so proud of you guys," Mandy says. And Kirsten pins a round piece of paper on my shirt. It says, "Good job" in gold glitter. I'm wearing my favorite sweater, the green one I got at The Gap, and I hope the pin isn't making a hole.

Kirsten pats the sign, pats my chest. "You did great, Ben."

"Thanks," I say. I wonder what they'd do if we'd actually won.

I wear the sign until halfway through my first period keyboarding class. Then I pin it to Stacey Waller's backpack when she isn't looking. Sean Kotowolski, the freshman quarterback, sees me and gives me a grin. He holds up his foot. He's stuck his sign to the bottom of his shoe.

I keep my eyes open for the cat girl during passing period. I figure she's probably going to go to Willamette View. But there are something like a billion kids at this school, and I'm not really expecting to see her.

And then she walks into my third period Algebra II class.

And although I've wanted to see her, I've been looking for her, as soon as I do see her all I can think about is how she called me moron. All I can remember is the dirty look she gave me before she went into her house. I slide down a little in my desk, although you can't slide too far when you're as big as I am.

The cat girl sits down in between Joelle and Renee.

Algebra II is a required class. You have to have it to graduate in Oregon, so there's a mix of everybody, a few freshmen and seniors, a lot of juniors and sophomores. Joelle and Renee are sophomores. They went to the same middle school I did. In fact, I sort of had a crush on Renee, when I was in sixth and she was in seventh. Not that she ever knew.

The cat girl is talking to Joelle, and they're laughing about something. They look like they've known each other forever.

The cat girl looks different today. She has on a lot of dark makeup around her eyes. Now, in the light, I can tell that her hair's dyed, but it looks cool. She looks older than she did in the cul-de-sac. I'm not so sure she's my age. She could be a junior or even a senior. She says something, and Joelle and Renee both laugh. Maybe she's a sophomore.

Kyle Cameron and John Maybry walk in. They're both juniors. Kyle is the quarterback on the varsity team. John is a fullback. The varsity is doing really well. They've made the state play-offs for the first time in fourteen years. Just about everybody says hi to Kyle and John.

As he comes down the aisle, John bumps his hip against Matt Higgins's desk. Matt is a freshman nerd. I don't really know him, but I know nobody likes him. He carries a laptop computer around with him all the time. Now his books crash to the floor, and he just manages to save the computer.

"Dumb ass," Kyle says to John.

John shrugs. "It's not my fault they don't make these aisles big enough."

They both stop in front of my desk. Kyle points at me. "Good game Friday, Gearbutt."

John grabs me by the shoulders and pulls me out of the desk. He's about three inches taller than me, probably outweighs me by fifty pounds. He's honkin' huge. "Gearfart!" he shouts. "Two interceptions! My man!" He rocks me back and forth, then slams into me, hard, with his chest, like he would if we were playing together, and I'd just made a great tackle or something. I know about half the guys in the room are watching. I know they all wish they were me. But it still hurts like hell.

As soon as he lets go, I sit back down. Everybody is looking at us. Including the cat girl. And, for a second, I'm afraid she's going to come over and grab me, too. Only she'll shout, "Cat murderer!"

John and Kyle see the cat girl, too. John puts his arm around Kyle and points to Kyle's chest. "You want him," he says to the cat girl. "You know you do."

Kyle grins. The cat girl turns her stare on him. Renee leans forward and whispers something to her. Finally the cat girl says, "In your dreams."

John throws his head back and laughs, and after a second, Kyle laughs, too. "You don't know what you're missing," he says.

"Oh, I bet I do," the cat girl says.

Renee and Joelle laugh.

Kyle sits down in the desk next to me. John sits down behind me. Mr. Venner walks in. He's almost always late. He teaches computer graphics before this, and everybody knows he likes to flirt with the girls in that class, leaning over to point things out on the screen, trying to look down their shirts.

John smacks me in the back of the head. "You do the homework?"

I snap it out of my binder and hand it back.

Venner stands in the front of the room, peering down at a buff card. "I see we have a new student." He looks around the room. "Gail? Gail Mapes?"

Gail. The cat girl digs out a bottle of nail polish and starts painting her nails black.

"Gail Mapes?" Venner says again.

Just about everybody is looking at the cat girl now. It's not like the room is full of new girls.

Venner finally catches on. He takes a couple of steps down the aisle toward her. "Are you Gail Mapes?" Most teachers would say something about the nail polish, make some crack about how this is a classroom, not a beauty salon. But not Venner.

The cat girl makes one more swipe across her thumbnail. She looks up, slowly. "My name is China."

Someone near the front, in the nerd corner, laughs.

Venner looks at the card. "The card says Gail."

"Well, the card is wrong. My name is China." She looks over at Joelle. "I don't know what the problem is with this school. This *never* happened at my old school."

"You'd think the least we could do for a new student is get her name right," Joelle says, shaking her head.

"The least," Renee says.

"It's not the least I'd do," Kyle mutters. John laughs.

Venner is looking confused. It's still morning, and he already has big sweat stains under his arms, like his deodor-

14

ant quits on the way over here. "Well," he says, "we can certainly get your name right in this class." He pulls a pen out of the Dilbert mug on his desk. He scratches out "Gail" and starts to write.

"That's China with a *y* and two *n*s," the cat girl says.

Venner's pen stops. He looks up. "Pardon me?"

In the nerd corner, Amber Parks rolls her eyes and says, "Oh, give me a break." Amber does not like anything that takes away from class time.

"You know. Like the group? Foreign Relations with Chynna?" the cat girl says.

You can tell Venner has no idea what she's talking about. "The band?" She sighs. "It's C-H—"

"Y-N-N-A." Joelle and Renee and about five other people help her finish.

Venner looks down at what he's written. "That *is* an unusual spelling."

"Talk to my mother," Chynna says. She starts putting polish on her left thumb.

"How can your mother have named you after a rock group that is—at the most—four months old?" Amber asks. Amber reminds me of Daria on the cartoon show on MTV, only Amber's not as cute, and she's never funny, and she's a total suck-up.

Chynna is concentrating real hard on her thumbnail. "You," she says, "don't know my mother."

It's not really that funny, but just about everybody laughs. John and Kyle and Venner laugh the loudest. And I'm impressed. There aren't that many kids who can walk into a new school in November and, by third period, be totally cool.

15

Venner pulls out the book and starts talking about the next chapter. I check behind me. John is still copying my homework, his big arms circling the paper. John lifts weights all the time, and he has these incredible biceps. He has a tattoo on his right arm, a ring of barbed wire, and it looks like it's been pulled and stretched to fit around the bulging muscle. And then I realize it's pretty weird to be sitting there staring at another guy's arms. I turn around. I lean forward a little so I can see past Renee. So I can see Chynna better. She has her head bent over her nails. But suddenly, she looks up, looks right at me. And she smiles.

For a second, I can't get my face to work. I'm so surprised, surprised she isn't mad, surprised she remembers me. I finally manage to smile back.

But then I realize she's looking around me, past me, through me. She's smiling at Kyle Cameron, not at me. And he's smiling back.

I don't see Chynna for the rest of the day, but then, at the very end, she turns up in my last period Freshman English class. So she *is* a freshman.

She sits down in a desk a little behind me. We do the whole "Chynna with a *y* thing," although Mrs. Whitman doesn't even comment on it. She just hands Chynna a copy of *Fahrenheit 451* and says, "I'm handing out packets. You can work on them in groups of three or four."

Jeremy shoves his desk across to touch mine. "I'll help you out with this, Ben."

I was sort of hoping this girl named Megan Frasier from the girls' varsity soccer team would work with me. But I see her sit down with Ty and Jenna and some girl I don't know.

So I say, "Thanks a bunch, Jeremy" just as Chynna plops into the desk Amber Parks has emptied behind me.

"I'll work with you guys," Chynna says.

Jeremy gives her a look, but when I angle my desk around to face her, he moves his, too. He opens up his packet.

"So," I say. I try to keep my voice light, easy. "How's your cat?"

Chynna gives me this blank look, like I've gone nuts. Then she waves her hand. "Oh. Oh. Actually, he's okay. He was just stunned or something."

"No kidding?" And I'm glad, really glad. Only I'm a little ticked, too. She could have told me sooner. She could have walked across the street and told me, so I didn't spend all weekend feeling bad.

"He's a great cat. He eats cantaloupe. But it gives him really bad gas." She giggles.

Chynna Mapes does not look like the kind of girl who would giggle much. I laugh. Jeremy frowns.

"So. Are you a Christian?" Chynna reaches out with her pencil and taps the bracelet on Jeremy's wrist. I hadn't noticed it before. It's a hemp bracelet with little plastic lettered beads: W W J D.

"Of course I'm a Christian." He looks at me. "You know Angie Betts?"

"Uh . . ."

"She's in my math class. She went to Hatfield, too. She's trying out for the dance team."

"Oh. Sure." I have no idea who this girl is.

"She invited me to this lock-in thing at her church on

Friday night. And they were making these bracelets." He shrugs. "And I got one."

"You were locked in a church overnight?" Chynna asks.

Jeremy sighs. "It was a party, actually."

Chynna reaches out with her pencil again and taps each bead. "'What Would Jesus Do?' I don't get it."

"There's nothing to get," Jeremy says. "It's just like . . . well, like if someone tried to sell you drugs. You ask yourself. 'What would Jesus do?'" Jeremy's voice hasn't changed yet, and sometimes he still sounds like a little kid.

Chynna looks from me to Jeremy and back at me. "But that's dumb. Who in their right mind would offer Jesus drugs in the first place?"

I laugh. "I've never thought about it that way."

"That's because it's a stupid way to think about it," Jeremy says.

Chynna shrugs. She flicks the front cover of her copy of *Fahrenheit 451*. "I've never heard of this. What's it about?"

"Book burning," I say. "In the future. It's science fiction, I guess."

"In Seattle we were studying Kurt Cobain and his music."

"Now there's great literature," Jeremy says.

Chynna ignores him. She points to the picture on the front of the packet. "And what is *that?*"

Mrs. Whitman has drawn a wolverine and written, "Beat Ashland!" on the front of the packet. She does that kind of thing all the time. "It's supposed to be a wolverine," I say. "You know. The Willamette View Wolverines?"

"Of course, you probably didn't have a football team in

18

Seattle," Jeremy says. "You probably just had a grunge rock group."

"As a matter of fact, we did," Chynna says. She looks at me. "I thought Wolverine was that guy in the X-Men comics. You know, the guy with fingernails." She sticks out her own fingers and waggles them in my face.

Actually, I'm sort of impressed she knows about the X-Men. But Jeremy laughs so loud and so nasty, I don't say anything. Mrs. Whitman looks over at us. Chynna immediately clamps her hand over her left eye. "My contact's slipped off. Can I go fix it?"

When Mrs. Whitman says yes, Chynna gives Jeremy and me a big smile. I don't think she's even wearing contacts.

Jeremy watches her walk toward the door. "Whoa. Is she dumb or what?"

"She's not dumb. She's just . . ." I can't think what Chynna is. And I'm not sure why I'm defending her.

"I heard that she was expelled from her old school," Jeremy says. "Up in Seattle."

"Who told you that?"

"I don't know. I just heard it. She was stoned, and she set fire to the bathroom."

We both look at the door, then we look at each other. "Everybody's saying it," Jeremy says.

I shrug and open my packet. "People say a lot of things, Jeremy."

"Yeah," Jeremy says. "But some of it's true."

# Chapter Three

$M$r. Parsons calls that night. He's my Global Studies teacher and the freshman football coach. "Hey, Ben. How's it going?"

"Okay."

"Bet you miss those practices in the rain and the mud." He laughs.

"Yeah. Right," I say. Only I do sort of miss the practices. It's weird to just come straight home after school.

"Look. The reason I'm calling? There's going to be a pep rally on Friday. For the varsity team and the game on Saturday against Ashland. And they're going to do a thing for the freshman team. Just a little appreciation thing."

I groan. This sounds totally humiliating. "Do we have to be there?"

Mr. Parsons laughs again. "And wear your jersey, okay? I'll be collecting them right after the rally."

I don't talk to Chynna at all the next few days, not at home and not at school. But I watch her. I watch her laugh at something Kyle says in algebra. I watch her eating lunch with Joelle and Renee and a bunch of other girls. At home,

I watch her go out to pick up the mail from their mailbox. I watch her have an argument with her mother in the middle of the driveway. Back at school, I watch her stop Kyle in the hall and ask him for directions or something. I watch him watch her walking away.

Friday is a really long day. People keep asking why I'm wearing my jersey. They ask how the freshman team is doing, how many more games we have to play. At the pep rally, they make us all stand up in a row. Mr. Vickers, the principal, calls our names and gives us certificates that someone printed out on the computer. The band plays "We Are the Champions," which makes Sean and Chris and me totally crack up, and Mr. Parsons gives us dirty looks. I'm glad to turn in my jersey at the end.

I have Intro to Business after the rally. I decide to cut through senior hall, where they all have their lockers, and through the commons. It's longer that way, but not as crowded.

There's a line of big glass cases on the far wall of the commons, across from the reception office. Each sport has its own case. There's a big sign running across the top of all the cases: WOLVERINES ARE WINNERS.

Kyle is standing in front of the football case. "Hey, Ben," he says.

"Hey, Kyle."

He points inside the case. "Maybe we'll add a trophy this year. Right there. A big one. Right in the middle. Wouldn't that be cool?"

"Yeah," I say. "Yeah. That would be great."

He points again. "That's your dad, isn't it?"

In front of one of the biggest trophies, there are team

pictures. The winning teams of 1969 and 1970 and 1971. Dad is always standing in the back, his helmet off, his hair slicked back by sweat. He's grinning, and he has his arms around two guys on either side of him. Grandpa is always standing at the end of the row, his arms crossed. He's squinting at the camera, not even smiling. "That's my grandfather, too," I say. "On the end. The coach."

"I know," Kyle says. "He was coach here for like thirty years." He leans closer to the case. "You kind of look like him. Your grandfather, I mean." He grins. "Of course, you've got more hair."

"Thanks a lot."

Kyle straightens up. "It must be kind of cool, though. To have all that history. To know you're carrying on a tradition."

I think about it. About the family history. "I just like playing football," I say. And it's true. I like playing a lot. And I'm not letting anything ruin that.

"Well. It's a good thing you like it. Because you're going to be playing it for a while." Kyle gives me a punch. He doesn't hit as hard as John. "I gotta go. See you around."

I stand there by myself, staring at the picture. Back in May, Dad said, "I've known for a long time." I look at him, grinning, hugging those two guys. Did he know in high school? Did the other guys know? Mr. Yamaguchi is there, kneeling in the front row, laughing. Did he know? He has his arm around the guy next to him. Maybe the whole team was that way. Maybe the winning teams of 1969, 1970, and 1971 were all . . . I press my forehead against the glass. The whole thing sort of makes my head ache.

I'm late to Intro to Business.

Mom has left a snack for me on the counter when I get home. A bagel and an apple and some granola bars. I eat the bagel and the granola bars. The apple looks funny. I put it back in the fruit bowl. Now that I'm not working out regularly, I know I'm going to have to start watching what I eat. Not that I'm fat. But Kyle is right. I do look like Grandpa. When I knew him, he was really tall and really, really fat.

But I'm still hungry, so I grab three bananas out of the bowl and the jar of peanut butter and a spoon and carry them into the family room. I plop down on the couch and click on the TV. It's an old cartoon show, one of my favorites when I was like five or six. I put my feet up on the coffee table, peel one of the bananas, and spoon a dollop of peanut butter onto the end.

I'm starting on the second banana when I hear a loud, high-pitched yapping outside.

Schottsie!

I leap up and head for the front door. A piece of banana splats onto the floor, but I can't stop to clean it up.

Schottsie is the McKays' stupid little dog. For some reason, he has to poop in our front yard. And I'm the one who has to clean it up.

I dash out the front door, screaming and yelling and waving the banana above my head.

Schottsie freezes in the middle of the lawn.

"If you poop on that grass," I scream, "I'll kill you!" I rush at him, shrieking. Schottsie takes off through the hedge and back into the McKays' yard. Then he turns around and yaps at me.

"I mean it!" I shout. "I'll rip out your slimy little dog guts!"

Chynna is standing by her mailbox, staring at me.

I realize I still have the banana above my head. I lower my arm, slowly.

She shakes her head. "Wow. You really hate animals, don't you? First the cat. Now the dog."

"I just hate that dog," I say.

She nods, but she doesn't look like she believes me. She leans over, checks inside the mailbox, then clangs it shut. "I'm locked out. And I can't figure out where my mother hid the friggin' key."

"Oh. Have you tried the doormat? Or . . ." My brain goes blank.

"I tried all that." She wraps her arms around herself. She's wearing a short red dress with short sleeves. Her arms are long and skinny and very white against the red of the dress.

"Maybe there's a window open. . . ."

"Look. I'm friggin' freezing out here. Why don't I just come over to your house?"

She doesn't wait for me to answer. She starts across the street. She's got on white tights and black work boots. They make her feet look really big, and her legs rise up out of them like the sticks on Tootsie Roll pops.

When Mom finally decided that I was old enough to come home by myself after school, that I didn't have to go to Mrs. Connoly's where it always smelled like pork chops and baby piss, one of the rules was that I couldn't let anybody in the house. Friends could come over, and we could play outside, but nobody could come in the house.

I think about that now, but it seems like a little kid rule. A fourth-grade rule. And this is almost an emergency. The sun is shining, but it's cold out. As Chynna gets closer, I can see the goosebumps on her arms. I can't leave her outside to freeze.

She follows me into the house, past the living room, into the family room. I scoop up the piece of banana and toss it across the kitchen counter into the sink. I toss the rest of my banana there, too, and the empty peel from the coffee table. I shrug toward the TV. "That was on. I wasn't actually watching it."

She sits down on the couch and picks up the last banana. She points it, like a gun, at the TV. "I *love* this show. Did you ever see the episode where the bad guy makes this drink that turns everybody into zombies?"

"Koo-koo kola."

"Yes! I loved that episode. I wanted to drink that stuff. I wanted to know what koo-koo kola tasted like." She grins at me, and, just for a second, she doesn't look anything like a junior or a senior. She doesn't look like someone who'd get stoned in the bathroom.

She peels the banana and sticks it into the open jar of peanut butter. It breaks off. She fishes the piece out, pops it into her mouth, and licks the peanut butter off her fingers. "How come you can drive?" she mumbles.

"What?"

She swallows, slowly. "How come you've already got your permit? How old are you?"

I know Kyle or John would sit down on the couch right next to her, but I sit on the piano bench. "I turned fifteen in August."

She nods. "You get held back?"

"I did kindergarten twice."

She nods again. "I won't be fifteen until next March. God. It seems like forever." She folds up the peel around the rest of the banana and puts it all down on the coffee table. "Do you play?"

"What?"

She grins. "The piano, bozo."

"Oh. No. My dad does. Did. He doesn't live here anymore."

"Divorced."

"Separated."

"My parents have been divorced for ten years." She splays out her fingers, showing me ten. "And you want to know what's weird?"

"What?"

"They've gotten back together. That's why Mom and I moved here. Because they're together again."

"Well. That's cool."

She shakes her head. "It's sick." She picks up the remote, starts clicking through the channels. "So. Is Kyle dating anybody? I mean, seriously?"

I'm still on her parents and moving from Seattle. "Kyle Cameron?"

She looks up at me, gives me a look. "Duh."

Kyle and Laurel Morgan started going together in their freshman year. Everybody at Willamette View knows that. Laurel is captain of the girls' varsity soccer team, vice president of the ecology club, tall and blond and beautiful. She and Kyle are, like, perfect together. Only everybody also knows that, back at the beginning of October, Laurel Mor-

26

gan threw a pudding cup in Kyle's face in the middle of the cafeteria. And they haven't been together since.

"I think he's going out with someone," I say. "Another junior. Kyle's a junior."

Chynna puts the remote down. She nods. "Joelle said he and this girl had broken up. But I figured you might know more. Seeing as how you guys are friends."

I'm not sure Kyle would say we're friends. But I nod. "Yeah. Well. He did break up with somebody. Only now I think he's interested in this other girl. This other junior. He talks about her a lot." I know I'm starting to blush. I've always been a bad liar.

A car pulls into the cul-de-sac.

"That's gotta be my mom. Finally." Chynna stands up, smoothes her dress. She picks up the peel with the half-eaten banana. "You going to the game tomorrow?"

"Yeah. I think so."

"Then I'll see you there." She tosses the banana across the counter and into the sink.

I stand in the living room and watch her walk across the street. I don't know why I lied to her about Kyle and another girl. It's not like I'm interested in Chynna myself. And then I think, maybe I *should* be interested.

Mom pulls into the driveway as Chynna disappears into her house. I hear the garage door open, her shoes clicking across the kitchen floor. She comes to the doorway. "Benjamin Gearhart. Why is the sink full of bananas?"

"Chynna did it," I say.

She frowns. "China?"

"The girl across the street? In the Lowerys' house?"

"Oh." I follow her into the kitchen. I think she's going to

say something about having people in the house, but she doesn't. She takes off her coat and hangs it over one of the stools at the counter. She never does that. She always hangs her coat up in the front hall closet.

"What's wrong?" I ask.

She looks at me. "Nothing's wrong." She has a really funny look on her face. Worried? Guilty? I can feel a little knot forming in my stomach, right above the bananas and the granola bars and the bagel.

I flash back on Dad and last May. *Ben. There's something I have to tell you.*

Mom picks up a sponge and starts wiping down the counter, although it looks pretty clean to me. "I called your grandmother today. From work. She's coming to visit us."

"That's it?" I laugh and blow out the breath I hadn't known I was holding. I sit down on a stool. "That's the big news? Well. It's cool. It's great." That's a lie. Grandma drives me crazy. "Where's she staying?"

"With us."

"With us?"

Mom's scrubbing hard at an invisible spot. "Just for a while. A few days."

"Why isn't she staying with Dad?" Let him listen to the stories about Grandpa and the golden days of high school football. Let him hear about the girl cousins and how great they are at writing thank-you notes.

Mom stops scrubbing the counter and looks at me. "Here's the thing, Ben. Your grandmother doesn't know."

"Doesn't know what?"

"Why your father moved out."

"What?"

She shrugs.

*Ben,* Dad had said. *Ben, I'm gay.*

I just sit there, staring at her. "Why does she *think* he moved out?"

"He told her he's having a midlife crisis." Mom smiles, a funny, tight little smile. "And he told *me* he didn't think she could stand the truth."

*I'm gay.*

A midlife crisis. Why couldn't he have told me *that?* It would be much easier. So much easier. You can tell other people that. You can tell other people, oh, my dad is having a midlife crisis. You can't tell them he's queer. You can't tell them he's living across town with some guy named Keith.

Mom sighs again. "So. Anyway. I just wanted to warn you. Before Grandma gets here."

I close my eyes, open them. "When's she coming?"

"Next week." She looks around the kitchen and family room. "And this place is a pit."

I think about Grandma not knowing. "Did you know?" I ask.

She looks at me. "Know what?"

I make a face. "That he . . . that Dad . . ." I wave my hand. "Before he told us?"

She shakes her head, sighs. "I knew . . . well, I knew we had problems. I knew that sometimes he wasn't very happy." She sighs again. "But I never guessed why."

I nod. It actually makes me feel a little better. Knowing I wasn't the only one. Knowing I wasn't totally stupid.

# Chapter Four

Because the varsity team has made it to the playoffs, their game is downtown at the Civic Stadium on Saturday afternoon. Sean Kotowolski calls in the morning and says his dad will give me and Chris a ride. I'm glad to get out of the house. Mom is on a cleaning rampage.

At the stadium, Sean's dad sits with some parents near the exit to the snack stand. Sean and Chris and I sit with a bunch of other guys from the freshman team near the middle of the Willamette View cheering section. Sean takes off his hat and his sweatshirt. He's dyed his hair purple, and he's painted his chest with a big *W.*

"Whoa, mama," Chris says, and he laughs.

"You're gonna freeze," I say.

Sean shrugs. "I'll jump around a lot."

Ashland has a good team, too, and it's a pretty exciting game. By halftime, I've almost lost my voice from yelling. We all stand up to cheer as the team leaves the field.

Sean turns to me. "God. Wouldn't you like to be out there with them?"

I shrug. Actually, it looks like kind of a rough game. Lots of big hits. I can imagine how the guys feel, making some of those tackles. The bruises and the aches. I rub my own shoulder, just thinking about it.

"Yeah, well, Ben *will* be out there. Next year," Chris says.

"Says who?" I ask.

"Everybody," Chris says. He looks at Sean, and Sean nods. "Everybody knows you won't play JV. You'll go straight to varsity."

"It's because so many of the defense are graduating," Sean says. "And the JV defense sucks." He grins at me. "So don't let it go to your head. It's not like you're that great, Gearbutt."

"Yeah. Right." It sort of ticks me off when he calls me that. It's not like he's Kyle or John.

"But of course the varsity won't be needing a new quarterback," Chris says. "They already have a great quarterback. They don't need two of those." Sean gives him a dirty look, but Chris turns to me. "Let's go get a Coke and check out the girls at the snack bar."

I appreciate what he's doing, taking my side against Sean. But I don't have any money. "I'm not really thirsty. I think I'll stay up here."

Sean goes with Chris. I sit back and put my feet up on the seat in front of me. I'd never really thought about going straight to varsity. But Sean is right. The JV defense does suck. Half those guys aren't ready for varsity.

And then I think I spot Megan Frasier, down near the railing, standing with some girls. And I'm thinking it would be a great time to just kind of go up and talk to her. Just kind of go up and say, "Hey, I'm Ben Gearhart. I'm in your

Freshman English class." But before I can move, Chynna sits down in the empty seat beside me. "How's it going?"

"Okay." She's wearing really baggy jeans and a green sweater. You can see her belly button in between the bottom of her sweater and the band of her jeans. She's gotta be cold, and I realize I've never seen her wear a jacket. Maybe people in Seattle don't own jackets. She's also wearing one of those black dog collars with the silver studs.

She points down at the field. "I can't believe they do that in public."

The band is playing down there, but it's hard to hear them over the noise of the crowd. I see Jeremy swinging his clarinet from side to side, the plume on the top of his hat waving around. He looks like he's really getting into it. He looks pretty goofy. "They're actually a lot better than they used to be," I say.

Chynna shakes her head. "Hard to believe." She turns toward me. "Look. Tell me what Kyle did that was great in this game."

"What?" Kids are milling around. I can't see Megan anymore.

"You know. Tell me what Kyle did great so I can tell him when I see him on Monday." Chynna leans toward me, and her belly button disappears.

I take my feet down, and I lean forward, my head on one side. I try to act like I'm thinking hard, only I'm really trying to see her belly button again. I think it's an innie. "Well. That pass he made to Drucker? That was a great pass."

She nods. "Okay. Got it. What else?"

"The pass he got off just before the half ended. When they almost sacked him? That was good, too."

"You mean when all their guys knocked him down?"

"Yeah. It was pretty amazing that he managed to find anybody. And then, you know, when Evans caught it—"

"Okay, okay. Give me one more."

I tip my head further. Definitely an innie. "Well. When he ran it himself. You know? In the first quarter? That was a crucial down."

"Crucial down, crucial down, crucial down." She mutters it, with her eyes closed. Then she looks at me, suddenly. She has on glittery eye shadow. It makes her eyes look really blue. She counts off on her fingers. "The pass when he was being sacked, the crucial down, and the pass to Trucker."

"Drucker." I'm thinking Kyle would hate the dog collar. Laurel Morgan never wears stuff like that.

"The pass to *Drucker*," Chynna says. "Great. That should be plenty." She frowns. "You know, I was talking to Joelle, and she's never heard of this junior."

"What junior?"

"The one you said he's interested in. Kyle. The one he talks about all the time."

"Oh. Oh, her." I shrug. "I don't think a lot of people know about her."

"But you think it's serious?"

"Could be."

"Okay. Well, thanks." She stands up and starts down the steps.

Sean and Chris come back. Chris has a Coke for me.

"Who was that?" Sean nods toward Chynna. She's going down the steps slowly, probably because of the heels on her sneakers.

"Chynna Mapes? She's in a couple of my classes. She just moved here."

"From Seattle," Chris says. "I heard she got expelled for—you know—" He blushes a little. "Doing it. With a guy in the band room."

"A band guy?"

"That's what everybody says."

Sean nods his head. "Yeah. I heard that too. Right in the band room. She has a thing for band nerds."

"Well. She's hanging out with the jocks at Willamette View." And I'm sort of hoping that maybe they'll think I'm talking about me.

Sean grins. "Yeah. I heard Kyle's already made his move."

Chris nudges me sharply in the ribs. Angie Watkins walks by, and we all shut up and watch.

Chris leans over. "She's in my P.E. class. We had to run the mile yesterday, and all the guys were circling back so they could run beside her." He looks at me and Sean. "Watch her bounce, you know?"

"We know, numbnuts," Sean says.

Chris grins. "Heyer was so ticked. Nobody ran faster than like an eleven-minute mile." He shakes his head. "Now we have to do it again on Monday."

"I heard Angie and John Maybry cut third period yesterday. Went and had lunch at Angie's house." Sean raises his eyebrows. "John was probably helping her with her running."

Chris and I laugh, although I'm not sure why.

Sean looks at me. "That's part of being on the varsity

team, you know. Girls. Lots of girls." He punches me. "No virgins on varsity."

"Oh, yeah. Right." I can feel the blush, hot in my face. "That would be a great sign. For Leadership to make." I laugh, but Sean and Chris don't.

"I'm just telling you what I hear," Sean says.

"I heard they keep count," Chris says. "You know. Who has the most."

"But it only counts after you're on the team," Sean says, "so don't knock yourself out, big guy." He laughs like a maniac.

I try to hit him, but I miss and get Chris instead. He shouts, "Hey!" and takes a swing at me. I manage to punch Sean's arm. A Coke gets spilled. We're laughing so hard, we nearly miss the team running back on the field.

We win, finally, 21–14. I'm really glad for Kyle and John. I can imagine how they feel. How great it must feel to play on a good team. To know you're a good player on a good team.

When I get home, Mom's on the phone. "Oh," she says. "Here he is now." She hands me the phone. "It's your dad."

"Hello?"

"Ben!" Dad says. "Long time no hear from."

"I guess." I can't remember the last time I actually talked to him, instead of just listening to his voice on the machine. Now I wait to hear what new plan he's come up with. Back in August, he asked me if I wanted to go out on the river and try out a Jet Ski. In September, he asked if I wanted to go to the Winter Sports Show at the Coliseum, maybe we could buy me a snowboard.

He's always trying to think of things we can do together.

And I always act like I'm going to say, yes, sure. Act like I'm seriously considering being seen with him. And then I come up with some totally lame excuse. It's sort of fun.

He clears his throat. "That was some game last week."

At first I think he means a game on TV. I don't even watch the games on TV anymore, and it sort of makes me mad that he doesn't know that. But I say, "Yeah, it sure was. Some game."

Mom is scrubbing a bowl at the sink, scraping at the dried out Ramen noodles I had for lunch.

"A real bruiser," Dad says.

"Yep," I say. I look at my watch. "Gee. You know, it's almost five o'clock . . ."

"But you had some nice plays," he says, fast, before I can brush him off.

"*I* had some nice plays?"

"You sure did. That block in the third quarter? You anticipated the play. Waited to make your move. That guy never knew what hit him."

All of a sudden, it hits me. "You were *there?* You were at my game last week?" Mom looks over at me, and I turn around and face the cabinets. "You were at my school?"

"Well. Yeah." He gives a little laugh. "Although I got there late, and somehow I ended up on the wrong side of the field. I was standing with the Beaverton fans. Let me tell you, I felt pretty uncomfortable."

I press my forehead against the cabinet. I want to ask him if Keith was with him. And I am so glad Mr. Yamaguchi didn't see him. Didn't try to talk to him. Or them.

"Ben? Are you still there?"

36

I push my head harder against the cabinet door. I'm going to have wood grain marks on my forehead.

"Ben? Is something wrong?" He's got this touchy-feely tone in his voice. "No one saw me, Ben," he says quietly. A totally sensitive guy voice.

"Nothing's wrong," I say, a little louder than I mean to. "Everything's fine. It was a great game."

Behind me, Mom starts running water.

"Look," Dad says, and his voice is louder, too. Stronger. "The reason I called is I was wondering if you might want to go rock climbing."

We used to talk about it. Back before May. "Rock climbing," I say, and I turn around and face Mom.

"Yeah," he says. "I've been going to that indoor gym in Lake Oswego. They've got a great wall there. I've mostly been working out, lifting some weights. I haven't tried the wall yet, but it looks like fun." He pauses. I know he's tugging at his mustache. "It would just be you and me," he adds.

"Rock climbing," I say again. I'm trying to get back into the mood. Into leading him on. "When?"

"Well." Just on the one word, his voice lightens, gets a little higher. "Well. How about next Friday night? They have classes for beginners on Friday nights."

"Next Friday night? Let me check." And I actually look at the calendar hanging on the pantry door. I actually check the square for next Friday night. "Oh, gee," I say now. "I can't next Friday. I . . ." I told him I couldn't go Jet Skiing because of football practice. I told him I couldn't go to the Coliseum because I had a ton of homework. "I have a date."

There's a loud clatter. Mom's dropped something in the sink.

"A date?" Dad says. He sounds really surprised, and it ticks me off. This is so hard to believe? That Ben has a date?

"Yeah," I say. "A date."

"Anybody I know?"

Like it's any of his business. "No. Nobody you know."

"Ah. Well. That sounds pretty important."

"It is."

"Okay." More mustache tugging. "Maybe another time. Maybe we can get together some other time."

"Sure," I say. "Some other time." And I hang up.

Mom puts the bowl in the dishwasher.

"Did you tell him about Grandma?" I ask.

"I didn't have time." She turns around. Her hands are dripping water. "A date?" she says. She says it like she might ask about the weather. Like it's not really important that she know.

And I can't tell her I was lying. It'll sound too crazy. She'll ask me if I need to talk about this. I shrug. "Not a date, exactly. Just . . . just a thing."

"A thing." She nods. "Who with?"

I think about it. "Chynna," I say, finally. "Chynna Mapes. The girl across the street?" I point at her hands. "You're dripping on the floor." And I leave and go to my room.

# Chapter Five

I expect Mom to bug me about Chynna for the rest of the weekend, but we hardly see each other. On Saturday night, Mom goes out on a date herself. Only like the second or third time since May. Not that I'm counting. On Sunday she goes to the gym for a long time, and then she spends the rest of the day working on the computer. That evening I watch *The Simpsons* and *King of the Hill*. Sometimes I think they're the most normal people on TV.

On Monday morning, she offers to let me drive to school instead of taking the bus. I know she's trying to make up for leaving me alone so much, and I think about saying no. Just to make her feel bad. But I hate riding the bus.

She nearly has heart failure when she thinks I'm going to run a red light, but otherwise, the drive to school isn't too bad. Fortunately we're early, and there's nobody around to see me pulling up with my mother in the passenger seat.

Except Kyle and Laurel Morgan are standing in the commons when I go inside. I can tell they're arguing, and as I get closer, Laurel says, "You just don't understand!"

She's wearing a tight black skirt, and her long blond hair and her hips sway in the same rhythm as she walks away.

Kyle watches her walk away, too, and he looks pretty sad. I'm starting to turn back around, thinking I'll just go outside and wait, but he sees me. "How's it going, Ben?"

"Okay." I can't think of any good reason to leave now. "That was a really great game on Saturday. You had a great game."

"Yeah. I guess."

"Well." I'm pretty sure I've got to get going, although I can't think where.

"You know what I hate?" Kyle says. "I hate that girls just never say what they mean."

I nod. "Yeah. I hate that, too."

"Last month, you know, she all of a sudden tells me she doesn't want to go to the homecoming dance. She tells me homecoming dances are stupid and boring." He shakes his head. He has zits on his neck, from shaving. "I like the homecoming dance. I mean, the first big dance of the year. You went, right?"

I nearly laugh out loud. "Sure."

"And it was fun, right?"

"Right."

He nods. "But I like Laurel. I like Laurel a lot." He looks really sad again, and I stare up at the banner hanging behind him. Another great Wolverine. This one's kind of smiley, not so fierce. "So I say, 'Okay, hon. We don't have to go to the dance. We can go to a movie or something instead.' And you know what she says?"

Outside there's the shriek and thud of air brakes. The buses are arriving. "What?"

40

"She says, 'No, no. I don't want you to miss the dance. Why don't you go with Jenny Whitaker? Jenny likes you.'"

He looks at me. "You know Jenny?"

"Sure." On the dance team. Junior class vice president. Breasts almost as big as Angie's. "She's pretty cute."

"I guess." Kyle shakes his head. Kids bang open the doors, and suddenly it's like a wall of noise hits us. Kyle steps closer to me and raises his voice. "So, like an idiot, I ask Jenny to the dance, and what happens?" He doesn't wait for me to answer. "Laurel's ticked off. Can you believe that? It's like it was this test. . . ."

"Not an algebra test, I hope." Chynna pushes her way in between us. She's wearing a tight white T-shirt and a tight black skirt, too. But she doesn't look at all like Laurel. She has on a lot of black makeup again. And the dog collar.

Kyle's staring at that collar. Then he grins. "Not an algebra test." He nods at me, doesn't stop looking at Chynna. "Actually, I was just telling Ben here what a pain girls are."

Chynna grins, too. "Oh. I can believe that." She puts her hand, flat, on his chest. "That was a great game on Saturday. The pass you made to Drucker was just amazing." She flicks a quick glance at me. "Wasn't it, Ben?"

"Pretty amazing."

"Well." Kyle is totally grinning now. He puts his arm around her shoulders, and his hand falls, easily, right next to her left breast. "Let's walk and talk together, and you can tell me more about me."

I'm standing there, like a moron, watching them walk off when John comes up and pounds on my back. "Hey, Gearfart!" Jerome Drucker and Jorge Rivas are with him.

"Weren't we incredible on Saturday?" John yells, and he

pounds me on the back again. I can hardly breathe. He puts his hands up above his head and turns around in a big circle. "Wolverines rule!" he shouts at the top of his lungs, and Drucker and Rivas shout, too. Kids look and laugh. Across the room, Brandon Lockley yells, "Friggin' right, man!" although Brandon's a doper and a loser and probably has no idea what he's shouting about.

John lowers his arms and grins at me. "After that play, you know, when they sacked Kyle?" He and Drucker both look at Rivas. Rivas spreads his hands and shakes his head. "Not my fault, man. I was covering Weiker." John snorts, but he turns back to me. "Coach said, 'Gearhart could have plugged that hole. We need Gearhart out there.' Isn't that what he said, Jerome?"

Drucker shrugs. "I dunno, man. I got hit bad on that play. All I remember is sparkly lights and bells ringing."

John puts his arm over my shoulders. It makes me nervous when he does that. I think he's going to hit me again. "I made varsity when I was a sophomore." He gives a really fake sob. "It was the best thing that ever happened." And then, suddenly, he grabs my head under his arm and rubs his knuckles, hard, through my hair. He pulls me up and says, "By the way, have you seen Kyle?"

"No," I say. I jerk myself free. "No. I haven't."

Kyle and Chynna aren't in algebra. John looks at Kyle's empty desk and at Chynna's. He grins. "That girl is hot," he says. Then he grabs my homework.

Chynna eats lunch at the varsity table with the guys on the team and the girls who hang around with them. She's there again on Tuesday and on Wednesday. I eat with Sean and Chris.

I'm home for about half an hour on Wednesday, doing my Spanish homework and watching an old sitcom, when the doorbell rings. Loud and long, like someone is leaning on the button.

Chynna's standing on the porch. "I was afraid you couldn't hear me. Like you were in the bathroom or something."

"I'm doing homework." I don't open the door too wide. I don't feel like answering questions about Kyle.

But she pushes the door open and walks in, walks right through to the family room. She glances at the TV. "What's that?"

"*Mork and Mindy?* It's an old show from like the seventies." I point at the screen. "See. That's Robin Williams. Before he was in movies."

"Weird," Chynna says. And I don't know if she means Robin Williams or the show or me for watching it. I click off the TV.

She sits down on one of the stools at the counter. She's wearing a blue sweater. It has little nubs on it that you sort of want to pick at. Mom has left me a box of brownies. The package says "low-fat" in big letters. "Ooh," Chynna says. "Can I have one?"

I push the box closer to her. "They're sort of gross."

She takes one, unwraps it, takes a little bite. "Low-fat's always gross," she mumbles. She swallows, wipes crumbs off her lips. Some of her lipstick comes off, too. "I bet your mom is dating again, right?"

"Sometimes."

"And I bet she's started working out. Watching her weight. And buying new clothes." She nibbles a corner.

I nod. I'm actually pretty impressed.

"My mom did the same thing. In fact, she did it, like, continually, because guys were always dumping her. Of course, now that Dad's back, she's given all that up. She eats constantly." Chynna puts the rest of her brownie down and shoves it away.

I reach out for the box. Watching her not eat has made me hungry.

Chynna grabs my hand. "Omigod. You have the nicest fingernails."

"No, I don't." I try to pull my hand back, but she's surprisingly strong.

"Yes, you do. Let me do your nails!"

"No way." I yank my hand free.

But she's pulling off the little backpack she wears, pawing through it, digging out lipstick and mascara and more lipstick and a pen, which surprises me. Finally she finds the little bottle of black nail polish. "Aha!" She pats the stool next to her. "Come on. Sit down."

"Chynna. Really . . ."

"Oh come on. Lots of guys do it. All the guys in Seattle do it." She pats the stool again and makes a little pouty face. "Please."

Guys do it at Willamette View, too. Some of the druggies and a few of the thespians.

Her lip sticks out even farther, starts to wobble. I sit down and hold out my hand.

"All right." She uncaps the bottle and pulls out the little brush.

"It comes off, doesn't it?"

"Oh sure." She takes my hand gently in hers and draws

the brush slowly along my thumbnail. "With remover. Or it'll wear off."

I nod. My hand feels so big, and her hand is so small. And soft and warm. The brush almost tickles, and the polish is wet and kind of cold.

I realize I'm breathing loudly through my mouth.

She strokes the brush one last time along the nail. She looks up, smiling. "What do you think?"

I take a deep breath, try to get my voice steady. "Great," I manage to say.

"Nine more to go."

I nod.

She starts on the next nail. She changes the hold on my hand, tightens it. I close my eyes. "I sort of have a favor to ask," she says.

"What's that?" My voice sounds strange and far away.

"I'm going downtown. On Friday night?" She moves to the next nail. "And I was wondering if you could come with me."

I open my eyes. "What?"

She's grinning, but focusing on my hand. "Yeah. I'm getting my belly button pierced."

"What?" I say again.

She finishes my little finger. She leans back, checking all of them. "It's something I've wanted to do for a long time. And it turns out that Joelle's older sister works at this place downtown. She does piercing." Chynna looks up at me. "Isn't that perfect?"

"Yeah. I guess it is."

"Anyway, Sherri—that's the sister—she said if I come at like six-thirty on Friday, she'll be there alone, and she'll pierce me. Otherwise, I need all this stuff." Chynna shrugs. "You know. Parental permission. Crap like that."

"That sounds . . ." Really stupid, I'm thinking. Only I say, "Cool. And you want me to . . . ?"

She extends my left hand and arm out to the side. "Wave that around so it dries. Give me the other one." She takes my right hand, starts on the thumbnail. "Sherri says the neighborhood is . . . well . . . she said I probably shouldn't go alone. And Joelle can't come." Chynna looks up at me through her lashes. "She has a date with Todd Weiker. Can you believe that?"

I shake my head. Then I nod. I wave my left hand back and forth.

"Joelle says she's bringing the condoms. This time." The glance again through the lashes. I know my face is turning red. I wave my hand harder. "Of course, I only believe like half of what Joelle says." She bends over my hand again. "So. Can you come?"

Part of my brain wonders why she's asking me and not Kyle. But the brush is moving across the nail of my index finger. "How do we get there?"

"The bus."

"The bus?" I try not to sound too shocked.

Chynna looks up at me and points toward the wall over the TV. "It stops somewhere over there. On Carolina. Joelle gave me a map thing. I have it all worked out." Her hand tightens on mine again. The brush moves across the next nail. Cold and wet. "Can you come with me?"

"Sure," I say. "Sure. Sounds like fun." And I realize that I *do* have a date for Friday night.

# Chapter Six

Mom notices the polish right away at dinner. We never eat in the dining room anymore. We're sitting at the counter, side by side. It's not like she can miss my fingernails. So I know she sees them. She just doesn't say anything. And I don't say anything. I've almost finished my skinless, broiled chicken breast when she cracks. "Is that fingernail polish?"

No. I dipped my nails in ink. "Yeah," I say. I hold up my hand. "Cool, huh?"

"How did you happen to decide to do that?"

"All the guys in Seattle do it."

She nods, like this makes sense. She takes a little bite of chicken. "I do have some polish remover. In the bathroom. In case you were wondering."

Actually, I can feel my fingernails all the time. They feel tight and stretched. They're driving me a little crazy.

She nibbles at her broccoli. "About this date thing."

"Oh. Yeah." I pile my chicken bones onto my broccoli. "Friday night."

"Friday night," she says. "And you're going with the girl across the street?"

"Chynna." I'm thinking fast. Going downtown to get her belly button pierced is not going to cut it. I neaten up the bones and broccoli. "We're going to a movie."

"Ah. Just you and Chynna?"

"Yeah." I look at her. "I *am* fifteen, Mom."

"I know, I know. And I'm glad you're going out."

She smiles at me, and I can tell she *is* glad. It makes me feel sort of funny. Does she think I'm a total loser?

She's still smiling. "So. What movie are you seeing?"

I need to concentrate here. I finish my glass of milk. I think about previews I've seen on TV lately. "We're going to try to see the new *Die Hard.*"

She nods. "And how are you getting there?"

A toughie. I'm thinking fast. I wish I could think this fast in algebra. "The bus," I say, finally.

"The bus?" She sounds almost as surprised as I did when Chynna said it.

"Yeah. We're going to the Washington Square Cinema. The bus goes right there." I know this because once, in eighth grade, when I asked Dad to drive me and Jeremy to the mall, he said we could take the bus. We decided to stay home. "You're always saying I shouldn't beg for rides, you know. Be more independent. Save gas." I'm on a roll now.

"So you'll be home early?"

How long can it take to pierce a belly button? "Yeah. Before ten." I'm not pushing my luck.

"Well. Sounds like fun."

I nod. "I think so." And it does sound like fun. Actually, it sounds like more fun than what we're really going to do.

I run into Jeremy on the way to the cafeteria on Thursday. I can't figure out how to ditch him nicely, so we end up eating together. He checks out my nails.

"A girl did it," I say.

He nods. "The Chynna girl?"

I shrug. I point to his wrist. The bracelet is gone. "What happened?"

"Angie? The girl from the church?"

"I remember."

"Turns out she's going out with this guy on the roller-hockey team."

"Bummer."

"I sort of wasn't into all that stuff anyway."

For a second, I'm not sure what Jeremy's telling me. And I must have a funny look on my face, because he says, kind of quick, "I mean all that church stuff."

"Oh. Right. That stuff."

Jeremy points at my nails. "So. Are you and Chynna going out?"

"No. She just comes over sometimes. She lives across the street, you know."

"You like her?"

And I think about saying that I just don't know. I think about saying that sometimes I think she's funny and nice. And sometimes I think she's weird and sort of nuts. And I know Kyle likes her. And John thinks she's hot. And I feel like I ought to like her. I *ought* to be attracted to her. And I want to ask Jeremy what he thinks.

But I know Jeremy will think I'm totally crazy.

"She's interesting," I say, finally.

He nods.

"Hey, Jeremy." Brandon Lockley is standing at the end of the table.

"Hey, Brandon," Jeremy says. "What's happening?"

Brandon grins. You can smell the pot on his clothes and his hands. He pulls his shirt up.

He has big safety pins stuck right through both of his nipples. "I did it myself. Yesterday, when I was suspended." The left one looks red and sore and scabby. A little drip of blood trails down from the right one.

"Whoa," Jeremy says. He looks at me. His eyes are really big and wide.

I put down my sandwich. All of a sudden, I'm not so hungry.

Jeremy squints at Brandon's left tit. "Doesn't it hurt?"

Brandon looks down at himself. "Sort of. A little."

"Only when you laugh?" Jeremy says, laughing.

Brandon shakes his head. "No. It doesn't hurt at all then. It hurt like hell when I did it." He pulls the shirt down. "Nice nails," he says to me. Then he takes off, probably heading to the bleachers to smoke.

I'm thinking about Chynna, about belly-button piercing. What if she gets some kind of awful infection or disease or something? What if it hurts so much she passes out? What if she bleeds to death?

Jeremy's staring at me. "You don't look so good. Are you okay?"

"Sure. Sure. I'm fine. How do you know Brandon, anyway?"

"He sits next to me in French. He's actually kind of funny. And he's smarter than you'd think." Jeremy opens his can of Coke. "I hope he was really stoned when he did that."

"I'm sure he was," I say.

That night I get out the remover and clean the polish off my nails.

On Friday at lunch I get two tacos and two bean burritos from the Taco Bell lady. I look for Sean and Chris, but before I can spot anybody, John comes up behind me. "Come eat with us, Beerhart."

We sit down with Kyle and Drucker and Rivas and Patterson, one of the nose tackles. No girls today.

"Cheerleader meeting," Kyle says, like I'd asked out loud.

Drucker pokes one of my burritos. Beans ooze out. "Glad I don't have any classes with you this afternoon, Gearbutt." They all laugh.

I almost ask if they've seen the movie *Blazing Saddles*. But it seems a lot to explain, the campfire scene and the beans.

Mr. Aronson, the drama teacher, stops by the table. "Hey, guys." Mr. Aronson has really white straight teeth, and his hair is always perfectly in one place. He's always dressed up, too. Vests and bow ties and baggy cords. Today he has on black jeans and a black turtleneck and a black jacket. "Big game tomorrow. I just wanted to wish you luck. I won't say break a leg."

Everybody laughs, politely.

"Thanks a lot, Mr. A," Kyle says.

"Yeah, thanks," the other guys say.

As soon as he's gone, Drucker makes a big deal of sniffing the air. "I smell something fruity," he says.

"They're all like that. All those drama people," John says. "And their club. The Lesbians."

"Thespians," Kyle says.

"Lesbians. Thespians. Same thing. They're all gay." He gives me a shove. "Aren't they, Gearbrain?"

"Yeah," I say. "Sure."

"And there's absolutely nothing wrong with that," Patterson says.

There's dead silence. Everybody looks at him.

"That's what they always said on *Seinfeld*. What's wrong with you guys? You don't watch TV?"

Rivas leans forward. "Did you hear about Tom Fitzgerald? You know? He's in speech?" Rivas looks like he has something smudged under his lip, but I think he's trying to grow a soul patch.

They all nod. I nod, too, although I don't know the guy. I'm not taking speech.

Rivas grins. "He tried out for the dance team."

"What?" John drops his taco.

"Yeah. He says he did it because they've been discriminating against guys. To make a statement."

"Oh, yeah. Right," John says.

"He didn't make it, anyway," Patterson says. "It's not that big a deal, John."

John stands up. "Fitzgerald!" he shouts at the top of his lungs.

A few kids turn and look.

"Come over here, you little fairy! I want to kick your little fairy butt!"

People laugh. Someone yells, "Shut up, Maybry!" Fitzgerald doesn't come over.

52

"Sit down, you moron," Patterson says. He's shaking his head. Drucker grabs John's arm and pulls him down.

Kyle is staring behind me. I twist around. Laurel is standing by the pizza counter, talking to a tall, skinny, blond guy. "Who's he?" I ask.

Kyle shrugs. "I don't know. I don't care."

Chynna walks up with Joelle and Renee. "Hey, guys." Chynna reaches over and takes Patterson's hat, puts it on herself backward.

"Hey there." Kyle grins and pushes back from the table. "How's it going?"

"Just fine." She leans over a little toward him. Kyle grins and puts his hand around her waist, and I see him glance, real quick, at Laurel.

Joelle is looking around the room. "Have you guys seen Todd?"

Patterson and Rivas exchange looks. Drucker clears his throat, but doesn't say anything. Finally, Kyle says, "I think he had a doctor's appointment." The rest of the guys nod, eyes big, smiling.

Joelle narrows her eyes. "Right," she says.

"I told you so," Renee says in a little singsong voice.

"We're cutting our next class to go over to Renee's and do our hair," Chynna says. She waggles her eyebrows at Kyle. "Want to come?"

Kyle grins, but he shakes his head. "I've got weight training next period."

Chynna glances at Renee and Joelle. They shrug. "Oh, well," Chynna says. She ruffles Kyle's hair. "Your loss." The three of them leave. Chynna still has Patterson's hat.

We all watch them walk away. And I think about telling

them about the trip downtown. That I'm going with her downtown. But I don't know if they'll just laugh. And I don't know if Kyle will get mad.

John leans over and smacks Kyle on the arm. "So. You guys weren't in algebra on Monday. Where did you go?" Kyle leans back a little and grins.

John counts off on his fingers. "Laurel to Jenny to Becky after the Halloween dance to Chynna. All in a month." He cups his hands around his mouth and makes a noise like a crowd cheering. "And he scores again." Patterson and Drucker laugh. Kyle grins even wider.

Rivas is shaking his head. "I think she's weird looking. Too much makeup. And where does she get those clothes?"

John snorts. "What's it matter? It still counts, even if you don't like the way she dresses."

"*I* like the way she dresses," Kyle says. "I think she looks . . ." He leans back even farther. "Exotic."

John laughs. "Yeah. I think she looks sexy, too."

Kyle reaches over and slaps him on the side of the head. "Exotic, numbnuts. Not erotic."

"Look out," Rivas says quietly, and he points over Kyle's shoulder.

Laurel and about four other girls walk up. Megan Frasier is one of them. The blond guy has disappeared.

"Guess what time of year it is, guys?" Laurel says. She manages to look at everybody at the table except Kyle.

They all groan. "Not again," Drucker says.

One of the girls drops a cardboard box right next to Kyle's tray. "Fund-raising time," she says, with a big grin. "We're selling candy bars for the choir."

"So fork over, boys," Alison Monroe sits down next to Rivas. "Support a good cause."

Laurel nods. "Seeing as how the football team never has to sell junk food."

"Or wash cars," the girl with the box says.

"Or do pasta wrestling," Megan says.

Everyone stares at her.

"You guys are gonna wrestle in pasta?" Patterson says.

"We're thinking about it," Laurel says. She frowns at Megan.

Megan looks at me. She shrugs and smiles. I run my tongue quick over my teeth, checking for burrito. Then I smile back.

"Well, I'll buy some." Kyle is digging out his wallet.

Megan leans a little toward me, and I can smell hot sauce. She ate Taco Bell, too. "Did you finish that English homework, Ben?"

"Yeah. Yeah, I did." I grin. She knows I'm in her class. She knows my name. "I didn't know you were in choir."

"Yeah. I'm not that great or anything." She shrugs again. She has a great shrug. "Want to buy some candy bars? We need new robes."

"Sure." I dig out a buck, all the money I have, and I buy one.

Kyle buys five. Laurel doesn't even smile at him.

Later, I see five candy bars in the garbage by the door to the weight room.

# Chapter
## Seven

I hang out in the weight room for a while after school. I'm thinking maybe some of the soccer team will show up. But the volleyball team has taken the place over. I work on my abs and biceps for a while, anyway. I end up having to ride the activities bus home.

But I still have almost an hour to kill before Chynna is supposed to show up.

Nothing much is on TV. An old black-and-white war movie and a Batman cartoon and some old geek from Broadway on the talk show on ABC. I go all the way up to Channel 62 and all the way back down. The best thing to watch is an open heart surgery on the Learning Channel. It's pretty gross.

The phone rings just as they're sewing the guy up. It's Chris. "Hey, Ben. You wanna go to the game with us tomorrow? The Barlow game?"

Like I don't know who they're playing. Like I didn't see the posters plastered all over the school. But I say, "Yeah. That'd be great."

"Okay. Sean's coming, too. Me and my dad will pick you up around one."

I hang up and go down the hall to my room. I've decided not to change my clothes. This isn't a real date or anything. And I'm wearing a pair of khakis Mom bought that I really like and a black long-sleeved T-shirt. My Doc Martens make me about two inches taller. I don't usually like the way I look, but this is okay.

I think about doing some homework, but then I flop down on my bed with my headphones and Discman and a CD Chris lent me about a month ago. "It's the kind you hate the first two or three times," he'd said. "But then you really start to like it. It grows on you." I've listened to it twice now, and I still hate it.

Now I get to about the middle of the second track. The guy is singing about some girl, getting it on with some girl. At least, I think that's what he's singing about. I close my eyes, and I think about no virgins on varsity. And I think about Kyle and Chynna going for coffee. And I'm wondering why she wants me to go downtown with her, why she picked me, and I'm hoping she's not going to spend the whole night talking about Kyle, when I hear a voice say, "Ben? Ben?" And for a second, I'm thinking it's the guy on the CD. For a second, I'm thinking, whoa, this *does* grow on you. Then I open my eyes.

Grandma is standing at the end of the bed.

I leap, and the headphones and Discman go flying. "Grandma!" I shout. I can't help it. She's scared me half to death.

"The front door was unlocked, so I came on in." She

reaches out and grabs my ankle and squeezes it. She has hands like lobster claws. "How are you, big guy?"

"Fine. Fine. Great." I scoot up on the bed, wiggle my ankle free. "How are you? How was your drive up here?"

"Couldn't be better." She looks around the room, then at me. "Your mom said you had a bad season. 0–9?"

"2–7," I say. "It wasn't . . ."

"I bet you don't have any offense. It's all in the drills, you know." She shakes her head. She has wispy hair that reminds me of cotton candy. White cotton candy.

"It wasn't totally the offense's fault."

"We know it wasn't the defense's fault. Right?" And she makes another grab for my ankle, but I shift out of the way. I think about telling her that I played defense *and* offense. But I don't.

She sits down on the edge of the bed. "You know what your grandfather always told his teams. There's always next year. And when the going gets tough, the tough get going. That's what he'd say." She smiles. "Not that he had many losing seasons. More wins than any coach in the district. More district titles. More state titles. A record that's never been broken." She points at me. "You know that?"

"I know it, Grandma."

"And that was your problem, I bet. Poor coaching. It always comes down to the coaching."

Mr. Parsons wasn't that bad. But he is a better Global Studies teacher than a coach.

Grandma smiles again, and I can see the flash of gold at the back of her mouth. "How's your mom?"

"Fine. Good."

"And your dad?" The smile fades maybe a little bit. No more gold. "You see him pretty regularly?"

"Oh. Well . . ."

"I don't know what's going on there. I'm here to try to straighten him out, Ben."

I open my mouth, but I don't know what to say.

The doorbell rings.

"I gotta get that." I scramble off the bed.

"Probably one of those Greenpeace people," Grandma calls after me.

It's Chynna. "You ready to go?" She's wearing a whole lot of black makeup, kind of curling up around her eyes. She has her hair shoved up under a floppy knit hat, and she's wearing a short black leather jacket. The jacket is open. Under it, she's wearing a T-shirt that says, "I go from zero to bitch in 2.5 seconds."

"Who is it, Ben?" Grandma asks behind me. I step aside.

"Well, you certainly don't look like Greenpeace."

Chynna looks at me. She raises her eyebrows. They look like two very black caterpillars crawling up her white forehead.

"This is Chynna, Grandma," I say. "We're going . . ." I nearly say "out," but I stop myself. Chynna doesn't think we're going out. "We're going someplace. Mom knows about it."

Grandma looks from me to Chynna and back at me. "Wear your jacket," she says, finally. "It's probably going to rain again." She leans out the door and peers up at the sky. Not that she can see much. It's dark already. "I certainly don't miss this weather."

"Grandma lives in California," I say to Chynna.

"Northern California," Grandma corrects me automatically. "I live in Redding with my sister, Viv. Redding is north of Sacramento. Not too far from the Oregon border."

Chynna has the look on her face she gets in English when Mrs. Whitman starts explaining something.

"We'd better get going," I say. I grab my jacket, quick, out of the front hall closet. Chynna has backed down off the porch. She's standing in the driveway, staring at Grandma's Saturn.

Grandma grabs my arm. I think she's going to say something about Chynna. Or ask where I'm going. But she just says, "Do you have any money?"

"Uh." Now that she mentions it, I don't.

She gets her purse off the table by the door. It's brown with a little magnetic catch. I used to love to play with it when I was little. I loved the little *snap* it made when the magnet hit the metal button. Now she digs out a crumpled twenty. "Here."

"Gee, thanks, Grandma. Thanks a lot." All of a sudden, I feel bad about leaving her. "Mom should be home really soon."

"Oh, don't worry about me. You just go out and have a good time." She pats my arm.

Chynna is hopping from one foot to the other by the time I get out there. "Let's go," she says. And she takes off, walking fast.

"What's the rush? It's barely even six o'clock."

She looks up at me, her face white in the streetlight. "I just want to be gone before my parents get home."

We reach the corner of our street and Sherman and turn

left. She puts her hand on my arm. "We can slow down now."

I realize she's sort of skipping to keep up with me. I shorten my stride. The top of her head comes to just below my shoulder. I feel really big next to her, big and clunky. I slow down a little more. "Nice jacket," I say.

She steps away from me, does a little twirl while we're walking. "Joelle lent it to me. Isn't it cool?"

"It's cool."

She jams her hands into her pockets. "Was that really your grandmother?"

"Yeah."

"Is she staying with you?"

"For a while. I guess." I don't really want to talk about Grandma. "Do your parents know you're getting pierced?"

She rolls her eyes. "They would pitch such a fit. But I really wanted to get out of there because it's Friday night. Family togetherness night." She deepens her voice. " 'Now that we're a family again, I want to make up for lost time.' " She groans. "Like I don't have a life."

We have to wait at Melanie Street for a bunch of cars that are turning. Their headlights sweep over us. Finally we can cross.

Chynna kicks a pinecone off the sidewalk. It bounces into the street. "He acts like we're supposed to pretend he hasn't been gone for ten years. Like everything is back to normal."

I think about that. About being back to normal.

"Do you know how much stuff I missed because I always had to spend weekends and vacations at his house?" She shakes her head. "Birthday parties and stuff like that?"

"Lots?"

She snorts. "Tons of stuff. And the losers they both dated? Melissa? Omigod. I hated Melissa. And Richard? Dick?" She says it in a really nasty way.

I laugh.

"Where does *your* dad live?" she asks.

"My dad?" I look down at her.

"Yeah. Is he here in town, or do you have to go visit him?"

"Oh. Oh. He lives . . ." Somewhere far away. I nearly say San Francisco, but that sounds too . . . "Chicago," I say.

Chynna nods. We cross Peachtree. "Was it another woman?"

"Who?"

"The reason he moved out. Did he fall in love with someone else?"

We're walking under some big old fir trees, and the light from the streetlights can't get through. She can't see my face. "Yeah," I say. "He fell in love with somebody else."

"Blond, I bet. And young. And perky."

"Perky?"

"Yeah. All the women my dad dated were always so . . ." She makes her voice high and happy and fake. " 'Oh, I'm so glad to meet you! You're so cute! You look just like your daddy!' " Her voice falls back down to normal. "And I'd think, 'Sweetheart, what *have* you been smoking?' "

I laugh. We're out from under the trees, back on open sidewalk. I think about Keith. I've never seen him, but I imagine him young and blond. Maybe kind of like that guy who used to be on *Saturday Night Live*. Definitely perky. I laugh again.

Chynna looks up at me. "What? What's so funny?" She tugs at my sleeve.

I shake my head. "Nothing. Well. You, I guess. You're funny."

We stop at Carolina, wait to cross. She still has her hand resting lightly on my arm. "I am funny, you know. But hardly anybody notices. They just think I'm . . ." She waves her other hand.

Slutty, I think.

"Weird," she finishes. "Everybody thinks I'm weird."

We cross and start up Carolina. She tugs at my sleeve again, like a little kid. "Do you think I'm weird?"

"No. No. I don't think you're weird." The bus stop is ahead of us, a little glass booth, lit up in the night. "Is that where we're heading?"

"Yes!" She grabs my hand, pulls me along the sidewalk. "Hurry up. I'm friggin' freezing!"

It starts to rain just as we reach the shelter. We duck inside. Chynna shivers. "This jacket doesn't have any lining." She steps closer to me. "Body heat! Body heat!"

And I don't know exactly what I'm supposed to do. Finally, I sort of rest my hands lightly on her shoulders. I think I should feel . . . I don't know . . . better about this.

Chynna smiles up at me. "You make a great bodyguard, Ben Gearhart."

"Thanks," I say. "Thanks a lot."

# Chapter Eight

The bus comes in just a few minutes. Chynna has to pay for me. All I have is the twenty Grandma gave me, and it turns out you have to have the exact change to ride the bus.

We sit in an empty seat near the middle. There's a couple of old ladies sitting up toward the front. A man is behind us. And three kids about our age are sitting in the back.

Chynna grabs the seat by the window. She checks out her reflection, wiping at something in the corner of her eye. I see my own face, floating round and pale above hers. I look away.

She gives my knee a shove with her knee. "You owe me bus fare."

"I know. I'll pay it back."

"No biggie. It's just . . . haven't you ever ridden a bus before? You don't give the driver a twenty."

I shrug. "I've only ridden the bus once before. When I was in preschool." And the teacher bought all our tickets.

"In preschool?"

"Yeah. It was this field trip. We rode the bus downtown, to look at the fountains and the statues and stuff. We rode the elevator in this bank building. To the twenty-sixth floor." I'm really surprised I remember all this.

"How come the twenty-sixth floor?"

"That's pretty high in Portland. We got out in front of this insurance office or something and looked out the windows at the river and the city." I can remember how excited we all had been, and I laugh. "A bird flew by, and it was, like, you know, just the coolest thing. To be up there as high as this bird."

Chynna has her back to the window, her knees pressing hard against my leg. She laughs now, long and loud. "Wow. Up there with the birds." I know she's laughing at me, but I don't care.

The bus stops. Two women get on and sit in the front seat, facing toward the driver.

"And then we walked over to Pioneer Square," I say, "and we looked at the statue of the guy with the umbrella, and we sat on the statues of the seals." I snap my fingers. "Oh, yeah. And there was this kid. Ryan Emberly? His mother wouldn't let him go on the field trip. She said downtown Portland was way too dangerous, and he was going to get shot by gang members or kidnapped or something. The next day we all told him how great it had been, and he cried."

"Oh, poor Ryan Emberly," Chynna says. But she laughs again. "His mother sounds even crazier than mine."

"Yeah." But I'm starting to think, what if Ryan's mother was right? Downtown Portland can be dangerous. You see stuff about it on the news all the time. What if we get mugged? Or shot at? What if we get lost? And I'm supposed to protect her.

Chynna gives me a shove with her knees. "Did you ever see that movie? Where the kids go to, like, downtown New York or something with their babysitter and get chased by drug dealers?"

"Yeah, yeah. *Adventures in Babysitting.*"

Chynna grins. "We had it recorded when I was little, and I watched it like a billion times. I used to want to do that. Go and have an adventure downtown." She leans forward, taps my arm with her finger. "And now we are. Only without the babysitter."

I watched that movie, too, when I was little. I'd thought it was scary. Lost in scary dark streets. Being chased by scary ugly guys who want to kill you. I shake my head. "That was Elisabeth Shue," I say.

"Who?" Chynna looks around, like we passed her or something. "Where?"

"In the movie. The babysitter. That was Elisabeth Shue. She was nominated for an Oscar for *Leaving Las Vegas* with Nicolas Cage."

Chynna leans back a little way from me. "You know the weirdest things."

"What do you mean?"

"Stuff like that. About movies and old TV shows and stuff. It just seems weird. You know. For a football player."

She's right. It is weird. It sounds like something Dad would say. In fact, it *is* something Dad would say.

The bus stops. The old ladies get off. A guy and a woman get on. They sit in the seat across from us.

Chynna grips my arm so suddenly it makes me jump. She leans back against me, her mouth pressed to my ear. "Look at that guy. Don't you think he looks like Kyle?"

I look at the guy across from us. He's talking to the woman, looking at something she's showing him in a magazine.

"I mean, when Kyle gets older," Chynna whispers.

"I guess," I say. "He's kind of bald."

Chynna leans back. "Kyle won't be bald," she says, loudly. Loud enough for the guy and woman to look at us. Loud enough for the women in front to frown. "But you're right. Kyle's way cuter." She stands up, as straight as she can in the seat. "Kyle Cameron is a hunk!" she shouts.

Everybody turns around. Everybody looks. The driver says, "That's enough of that." The kids behind us laugh. One of them sighs, "Ooh, Kyle," in a dopey voice. They're definitely younger than us. Probably eighth graders. The woman across from us leans forward and smiles at me. And I realize she must think I'm Kyle. I scrunch down in my seat.

Chynna sits back down. She's grinning.

"Did you have to do that?" I ask.

"Yeah," she says. "Yeah. I did."

We're stopping more often now, and I can see we're coming into the city. The houses are all really close together, and there are more stores mingled in between. We cross an overpass. You can see cars and headlights on the I-405 below us. And then we're passing office buildings and parking garages.

The bus stops in front of what looks like a record store. The kids in back get out. One of them moans, "Kyle, you hunk," as he walks past us. As they jump off, another kid yells, "I just farted in this bus!"

I laugh. I can't help it. Chynna's laughing, too. The driver gives us a dirty look in his rearview mirror.

"When's our stop?" I ask.

Chynna digs a crumpled note out of her pocket. "The Silver Unicorn Tattoos and Body Piercing. It's supposed to be on Second Avenue."

I peer around her, out the window. We pass a big hotel with a doorman in a red suit, just like on TV. We cross an intersection. "We're on Fifth."

"Joelle's sister said we should get off at Harding and then walk down toward the river."

Another block of buildings whizzes by. People and stores. It's stopped raining. A street passes, but I can't read the sign. "Was that Harding?"

"Yeah, it was," the guy who looks like Kyle says. The woman next to him smiles and nods.

"Really? Really?" Chynna looks around. "Damn." She grabs the cord and pulls it hard a bunch of times.

"All right. All right," the driver says. "Don't wear it out." He pulls over at the next stop. I'm a little afraid Chynna's going to yell something as we get off, but she doesn't.

We stand on the sidewalk as the bus grinds away from the curb. The air smells of diesel and car fumes and something heavy and moldy.

"Yuck. What is that?" Chynna makes a face.

And I remember, from back in preschool, Amanda Zuber making exactly that same face. "The brewery," I say.

"The brewery?"

"Yeah." I'm sort of proud I know this. I'm not a total suburban hick. Maybe I *can* get us around here safely. "It's the Weinhard Brewery. Up on . . ." I don't actually know where it is. I point behind us. "Up over that way."

"But we want to go this way." Chynna takes my hand and tugs me down the sidewalk.

We work our way back down to Harding. There are lots of people on the sidewalks, probably heading home from work. Everything is really well lit, and I'm glad to see so many people. It seems safer. Not at all like that movie.

There are fewer people on Harding, though, and the stores aren't lit up. A guy steps out from a doorway. An old guy, dressed in baggy gray pants and a ragged sweater. He needs to shave. "Got any change?" he asks, in a raspy voice.

I feel my heart jump into my throat. I know I can probably knock him down. He's just an old guy. I've knocked over much bigger and much younger guys. But what if he's got a gun? The opposing players never have guns. I grab Chynna's hand tighter, pull her around him.

She pulls loose. "Sure." She digs in her pocket, hands the guy some coins.

"Thanks." He lurches away, on up the street the way we came.

"You're not supposed to do that," I say, when he's far enough away he can't hear me. "He's just going to use it to buy booze."

Chynna laughs. "Oh. Like he's going to get drunk on fifty cents." She shakes her head. "Loosen up, Ben." And she starts walking again.

It is definitely darker and scarier the farther we go on this street. The buildings are almost all closed up. The windows and doors are covered with bars. We pass what looks like a dingy grocery store and a copy store. They're both open, but no one is inside.

At the corner of Harding and Third, there's an adult book store. The windows are covered with paper. The sign says FANTASY VIDEO AND BOOKS. FOR ALL YOUR FANTASIES. Chynna stops. "What do you think? Should we check it out?"

A big guy—bigger than me—in black jeans and a denim jacket comes out of the store. He mumbles something as he pushes past us.

I look at my watch. "Didn't you say you have to be at this place at six-thirty?"

"What time is it?"

"Six-thirty."

"Oh, hell."

The Silver Unicorn is about halfway down the block on Second. We see it right away. It has a big neon sign of a unicorn's head.

"Cool," Chynna says.

The windows are covered with pictures. I guess of stuff you can have tattooed on you. There are smaller signs that say HOSPITAL STERILE ENVIRONMENT and STATE LICENSED ARTISTS and SINGLE-USE NEEDLES.

"Did you ever see *The X-Files* where the guy has a tattoo that talks to him?" I ask. I can't stop myself. "It was Jodie Foster's voice," I add.

"Ben, Ben." Chynna shakes her head and goes inside. I follow her.

Inside there's a wide low desk and two chairs, with a coffee table in between them. There's a scraggly looking plant hanging from the ceiling in one corner. It kind of reminds me of a doctor's office, only the walls are covered with more tattoo pictures.

A woman comes through a door in the back, behind the desk. I figure this must be Joelle's sister, although she doesn't look much like Joelle. Her eyebrow is pierced. So are her nose and her belly button. "Hi, Chynna," she says. Her tongue is pierced, too. "Ooh. Nice T-shirt."

"Thanks," Chynna says. She looks at me. "This is Sherri. And this is Ben. My bodyguard."

"Hi, Ben," Sherri says. "We're having a sale today. Any second piercing for half price."

"That's okay," I say.

"Ear? Nipple? Navel?" She's ticking them off on her fingers. She has a spider tattooed on her ring finger.

"No thanks," I say, louder.

Sherri laughs. She looks at Chynna. "Well. You ready to do this?"

"Sure." Chynna glances back at me. All of a sudden, she looks not so sure. "Is this, like, gonna hurt?"

Sherri laughs. "Oh, no. I do this whole aromatherapy thing. It won't hurt at all. You know, you only feel pain if you expect to feel pain."

I nearly laugh. Clearly this woman has never played football. Chynna looks at me again. Maybe I'm supposed to stop her.

But she smiles. "Well. Let's do it, then."

Now Sherri frowns. "And you're sure it's totally cool with your parents? They aren't going to, like, sue or something?"

"They won't sue."

"Okay. I have to get it done before my boss gets back."

They disappear through the door.

I sit down in the chair. There's a *Sports Illustrated* on the coffee table. A really old *Sports Illustrated.* I'm sort of surprised. It doesn't seem like a magazine they'd have in a tattoo place.

I've looked at all the pictures, and I'm actually most of the way through a long article about Tiger Woods, when Chynna and Sherri come back out.

Chynna walks over to me, grinning, and pulls up her shirt. "Cool, huh?"

There's a small gold ring in the edge of her belly button. No blood. No scabs. It looks way better than Brandon's nipples. "Cool," I say.

"You're sure you don't want something done?" She leans over and taps my earlobe. "A stud?"

I clamp my hand over my ear. I can't help it. "I'm positive."

Chynna shrugs and pulls down her shirt. She pays Sherri from a wad of twenties she has in the little backpack.

Outside, she puts her arm through mine. "It did hurt. A little bit," she says. She pats her tummy. "Do you think Kyle will like it?"

I've never heard Kyle say anything one way or the other about pierced belly buttons. But I guess it's pretty exotic. "Sure," I say. "Sure. He'll love it."

# Chapter
# Nine

Chynna looks up and down the street. "So. What do you want to do now?"

I'd sort of been assuming we'd be heading home. Something—The Silver Unicorn or the smell in the air or the guy watching us from the window of the comic book store across the street—something is making me feel queasy. Like the time I ate seven hot dogs right in a row. "I don't know," I say. "What do you want to do?"

She walks down the street to the corner. I follow her. She looks down Harding. "We could go down to the river. I've seen pictures. There's a park down there or something, isn't there?"

Harding that way is very dark and very deserted. I can see cars crossing about two blocks down, but here, where we are, and all the way down to there, it's more closed office buildings and barred-up stores. "I bet it's cold down by the river." Behind us, the door to the comic book store opens, and the guy comes out. He has another guy with him. "Maybe we should head up, you know, back where the bus left us off."

Chynna pats her tummy again. "I'm starving." She points to a neon sign about half a block away. "Look. Chinese sounds good."

The two guys look like maybe they're thinking about coming over toward us. One of them says something, and the other one laughs. I think about Ryan Emberly's mother and about gangs.

"I don't want to eat anywhere weird. I think there was a McDonald's. Back on Fifth."

Chynna looks at me and rolls her eyes. "That's the spirit, Suburbia Boy." But she crosses the street and heads back up Harding, the way we came. I keep watch behind us, but the two guys aren't following us.

I relax once we get back to the brighter lights and the busier street. We have to push past people waiting in line for a movie theater. I try to see what's playing, but Chynna is walking too fast.

She stops at the edge of the sidewalk and looks up and down the street. "I don't see a McDonald's."

A car passes, really close to the curb. I pull her back. "Don't stand so close," I say. "It's not like—" I nearly say "home," but I stop myself. I know I sound like Pat, my preschool teacher. "I think it was back a ways," I say instead. "Up a couple of blocks." A bus goes by but doesn't stop. "What bus do we take to get back, anyway?"

Chynna shakes her head. "I think Joelle said we catch it on Bradley? Or Brooktree? No. That's a store. Something with a *B*."

My queasy feeling is coming back. "You don't know what bus we take to get home?"

"Jeez, Ben. You don't have to panic. It's not like we're . . ."

She pauses, looks around, then steps closer to me. "Lost in Portland, Oregon!" she yells, at the top of her lungs. She laughs, then points across the street. "Christmas!" She drags me out into the traffic, without looking or anything. One car stops for us, honking loudly. Another one veers around us. Chynna gives the driver the finger. Then she pulls me over to a stationery store.

Even though it's like weeks until Thanksgiving even, the window of the store has a big Christmas tree, full of ornaments that I guess you can buy there. Underneath the tree are boxes and boxes of Christmas cards. Two big dolls dressed in pajamas are standing under the tree, handing each other boxes of cards. Their eyes and torsos move back and forth, back and forth. They look really happy to be getting so many cards.

Chynna shudders. "That's kind of creepy."

"The Village of the Damned does Christmas," I say.

"Huh?"

"*The Village of the Damned.* It's this movie, an old one, with these scary kids. Only they're really from outer space. There was a remake with . . ." I stop. I'm doing it again. Only she isn't listening. She's opened her jacket and pulled up her shirt. She's checking herself out in the reflection in the window.

"What do you think? Do you think she should have done it over a little more?"

Two old guys in suits are walking behind us. They nudge each other and grin. "I think it looks fine."

She turns a little to one side. "I think I'll put in a bigger hoop, though. Once it's healed."

The men have stopped, are looking back. They look too

big to knock over. I reach over and pull down her shirt. "I thought you were starving." I grab her hand and pull her up the street.

We stop at the next corner. Directly across from us is a store with pots and pans and blenders in the windows. Kitty-corner is a big, open, bricked space. There are lots of people. Some are sitting on the benches under cold-looking trees. Some are leaning against the fake Roman pillars that run along one side. Some are just walking across the square, cutting over to the light rail station on the other sidewalk. A MAX train is just pulling up. A guy and a woman are sitting in the corner closest to us, under a metal statue of three horses running. The woman is playing a violin, and the guy is singing. Further on, some kids are beating on drums—or empty paint cans, maybe.

"Cool," Chynna says. "What is this place?"

"It's Pioneer Square." I point. "See. I told you there was a statue of a guy with an umbrella."

We cross the street. I make her wait for the light, cross in the crosswalks. We walk out into the middle of the square. It's paved with bricks with people's names engraved on them. "It's the people who donated money to build it," I say. "It used to be a parking garage or something."

Chynna nods, but I can tell she doesn't care. She's watching a bunch of street kids who have crowded around the drummers, clapping their hands and shuffling their feet to the beat.

"See." I put my hands on her shoulders, turn her around. "Look at that statue. Doesn't it look real? I mean, doesn't it look like a real guy walking along with an umbrella?"

"Whoa. It does." She laughs. The statue is at the top of some steps, and she runs up and stands next to it. She stands just like the statue, pretending to hold an umbrella over her head with one hand, while she sticks her other hand out like she's pointing at something. But she's watching the kids, too. I can tell she's hoping they'll turn around, see her being funny. I don't tell her that every kid in preschool did exactly what she's doing right now. Mom has the picture of me somewhere.

The drummers finish. There's a loud burst of laughter and applause. Chynna drops her arm, takes a step toward them. She's smiling, too, like she's already there with them. And I have a flash of the rest of the evening. Like a movie or TV show I've seen. She's going to start talking to those kids, and we're going to end up somewhere. Somewhere dark that doesn't smell very good. Maybe under a bridge. And there'll be booze and probably drugs. And I'll end up dead. I imagine the cops showing up to tell my mom. I *know* I've seen this movie.

Behind the statue, the MAX train pulls away from the station, and I see the golden arches glowing from across the street. "Hey!" I dash up the steps and grab Chynna's arm. "I told you so. I told you there was a McDonald's around here."

I tug her past the statue, off the bricks, and onto the sidewalk. People who've just gotten off the train are milling around with people trying to get on and people who are trying to buy tickets. A car honks. We'll have to wait to get through.

"But . . ." Chynna says. She pulls her arm loose. "Let's just go see . . ."

I step back, reach for her, and bump into a man trying to get by.

"Ben?" he says.

I look up at Dad.

It seems like we have a whole lot of time to just stand there and stare at each other. He's wearing his ratty old U of O jacket that Mom always bitched about. And his jeans are still too short, so his socks show above his shoes.

"Ben!" he says again. "Ben!" He puts out his arms like he's going to hug me, only then he lets them drop to his sides. He glances back at a guy behind him. "This is Ben."

The guy nods. He's as tall as Dad, only not as skinny. He maybe once had blond hair, but there's not much of it left. He's dressed kind of like Mr. Aronson. A sweater vest and turtleneck under a wool jacket. Baggy cords. He smiles and nods. Not exactly perky.

Chynna steps back up beside me. Now I wish she had gone over to the street kids. I wish she'd left with them. "Who's this?" she asks.

In about twenty seconds I run through about twenty lies. She has to be able to tell they're together. She has to be able to tell they're a couple.

"Hi, there." Dad sticks out his hand. "I'm Ben's father."

Chynna looks at me, and she looks at Dad. "No kidding," she says. But she takes his hand and shakes it.

Dad laughs. He has different glasses. They make his face look rounder. I don't like them. He steps aside a little, nods at the guy behind him. "This is my friend, Keith."

Friend, friend. Oh God. Did he have to say friend? I'm starting to turn red, the blood flooding up my face in a hot wave.

Keith smiles the most fake smile I've ever seen. He nods at Chynna, gives her a little wave.

Oh God. Don't wave like that.

"Well." Dad is still smiling. He keeps moving his hands up and down, like he doesn't know what to do with them. "You're so tall," he says to me, and he laughs again. "I can't believe how much you've grown since . . . when was the last time I saw you?"

"We gotta go," I say.

Chynna is frowning. "So. Are you like visiting here or something? I thought you live in Chicago."

Dad stares at her. "I live off Hawthorne. We rode MAX in to catch the movie at the Metroplex." He looks at me. "They've remastered *Treasure of the Sierra Madre*. The original. New tape. New sound." He grins. "Bahdges? Bahdges?"

And, for about a nanosecond, he nearly has me. Because I like that movie. I remember when we rented it and watched it with Mom. I nearly say, "We don't need no steenkin' bahdges."

But Keith says it first, and he and Dad both grin.

Chynna shakes her head. "That's not very nice. Talking like that. It's not politically correct."

Keith raises his eyebrows.

"You're absolutely right," Dad says, in a sincere, sensitive kind of voice that makes me wince. He's looking around, over my head. "Are you guys . . . Is anybody here with you?"

"No, no," Chynna says. "We're here by ourselves."

"By yourselves." And a look zips across his face, an old Dad look, from a long time ago. But then it's gone. "Well."

He gives me a funny, quick smile. "If it's okay with your mom."

"It's fine with her," I say.

"We came for this." Chynna pulls out her shirt and sticks her stomach out at Dad. "Pretty cool, huh?"

Dad takes a step backward, and Keith has to step back, too. "You came downtown to get your navel pierced?" Dad is looking at me, not at Chynna.

"Yep," Chynna says. "There aren't a lot of places to do it where we live. And this one down here is really totally clean."

"Sterile," I say. And I laugh. The look on Dad's face is too great.

"Don't you have to have an adult with you to do that?" Keith says. We all stare at him, like we're surprised he can talk. "I mean, I thought you had to have your parents' permission." He has a terrible voice. A swishy voice. He doesn't look like he'd have a voice like that.

Chynna waves her hand. "Oh, my mom signed this thing. Back before. Back last week."

Keith nods, but you can tell he's not convinced. I was right. I don't like this guy at all.

Dad is frowning at me. "You're sure your mother—"

"Grandma's here," I say.

Dad stares at me, his mouth still open. "Grandma?" he says finally.

I nod. "At our house."

Dad glances at Keith. "My mother's in town."

"I think she's going to give you a call," I say, although I don't know that at all. I just kind of like watching his eyes bug out behind his stupid round glasses. "You still starving?" I ask Chynna.

"Yeah. Yeah, I am."

"Well. We gotta go." I start to move toward the curb.

But Chynna stops. "You don't know which bus gets us back home, do you?"

Dad looks at me over her head. "You don't know how to get home?" I can tell he's thinking he should do something. He's thinking he should take us home. But he's thinking about Grandma, too.

Keith steps forward. "The number four. You catch it up on Broadway."

"Great," I say. "Thanks." And I pull Chynna toward McDonald's.

# Chapter Ten

I think Dad is going to follow us. To make sure we find the bus stop. Make sure we get on the bus safely. Him and Keith.

But we get into McDonald's, order our food, and grab a table near the back, and they never show up.

I rotate my head, trying to loosen the muscles in my neck and shoulders.

"How come you said your dad lives in Chicago?" Chynna asks as she unwraps her burger.

I stop rotating. "Oh. Well." I decide on a sort of half-truth, half-lie. "He kind of talked about moving there. I haven't actually seen him in quite a while."

"Probably a woman." She opens her burger and picks off the pickles. "My dad would always disappear when he had a new girlfriend."

Suddenly, I'm not so tight. "That's probably it," I say. And I realize I'm starving. I take a big bite of my Big Mac.

"Kyle eats his hamburgers absolutely plain. Did you know that?"

I take another bite. "Uh-uh."

She nods. "I went out with him last week. To the mall. It was fun." She puts the bun back on the burger.

I finish my Big Mac and shake out some of my fries onto my wrapper. "He's a pretty fun guy, Kyle." I'm feeling so much better, I don't mind talking about him. "I think he's probably going to attract some college recruiters. Next year, you know."

Chynna raises one eyebrow. "Right." She pushes the burger to one side. "He sort of reminds me of a guy I . . ." She pauses, picks up one of my fries. "Went out with. In Seattle. He was a junior, too."

"The band guy?" I rip open a packet of ketchup and sploodge it out onto the edge of the wrapper.

"What band guy?" She frowns. Then she smiles. "Oh. Oh. No. This was another guy. I met him over the summer. We were really close."

I don't know how she could get much closer than Chris said she was with the band guy. But I say, "You miss him?"

"Yeah. Well. I'm getting over it, I guess." She leans over and drives her fry, slowly, through the puddle of ketchup. "Joelle and Renee think Kyle really likes me."

I eat two more fries, lick the ketchup off my fingers. "Don't *you* think Kyle likes you?"

She shrugs. She's really coating that fry. "I don't know. He was so nice to me. That time we cut algebra and went for coffee."

I smile a little. Coffee? Is that what they call it in Seattle?

"Sometimes I just think . . ." She sighs and drops the fry. I can't believe she's not going to eat it. After all that ketchup. She looks up at me. "Do you think he likes me? I mean, really likes me? I mean, does he ever talk about me?"

I remember the conversation in the cafeteria. "Yeah. He talks about you." And all of a sudden, I think maybe I should warn her about Kyle. Maybe I should warn her about the guys on the team, keeping count of how many girls they make it with. Only I look around at the shiny tables and the bright lights. At the big plastic statue of Ronald McDonald, grinning in the corner. And I can't do it.

Chynna picks up another fry and starts with the ketchup again. "He did invite me to that party thing."

"What party thing?"

"At Todd Weiker's. Some football party." She grins, suddenly. "Although Todd did *not* invite Joelle, and she is totally ticked." She swirls the fry in a little red circle. "You ever been to one of their parties?"

I shake my head. Although I've heard about them. Even back in middle school, you heard about them, from kids with older brothers and sisters.

"I hear they can get kind of wild."

"Yeah. I've heard that, too."

She drops the fry and looks up at me. "I know! Why don't you come, too?"

I laugh. "Yeah. Well. Todd hasn't invited me, either."

She reaches out and grabs my arm. "I'm sure it'll be okay. Kyle's your bud. All the guys like you." She shakes my arm. "Come on, Ben. It'll be fun. And I'll feel better if you're there." She grins. "Remember. You are my bodyguard."

And who am I protecting her from? Kyle? Me? But I'm thinking about it. A party with the varsity team. It would be cool to say I'd been there. It might even be cool to actually be there. "I'll think about it," I say.

She grins and sits back. "Good."

I point at her burger. "You gonna eat that?"

By the time we leave McDonald's, it's raining again. Really pouring. Pioneer Square is empty. Only a couple of people are waiting at the MAX stop. Even the street kids have vanished. It's like everybody got flushed down the gutter with the rainwater. Chynna doesn't argue with me when I suggest we find the bus and head home.

Mom is waiting on the couch in the family room. She's wearing her pajamas and robe, even though it's only like nine-thirty. It seems like I've been gone a lot longer than that.

"How was the movie?" she asks.

It takes me a second. "Oh. Great. Really great."

She nods and smiles. "Have you eaten?"

"McDonald's." I sit down on one of the stools. There's a picture album open on the counter. I see a picture of Great-Aunt Viv in front of a casino and one of three blond girls sitting in front of a Christmas tree. "What's all this?"

"Oh. Your grandmother brought some pictures with her." Mom gets up and comes over to the counter. She taps the picture of the little girls. "Those are your Aunt Karen's kids. Boy, we haven't seen them in years. I bet you hardly remember them."

I remember them. The perfect girl cousins. "Where do they live now?"

"Anchorage."

I look at them sitting under their Christmas tree. I think about the Village of the Damned.

"Well," Mom says. "I think I'm going to head to bed. Now that you're home." She leans over and gives me a clumsy sort of hug. "I'm glad you had a good time, sweetie."

When she's gone, I flip through the picture album. Near the front there's a picture of Dad and me when I was about five. We're standing on the log dam at Timothy Lake. I'm wearing jeans and a flannel shirt, just like his. I have my arms crossed, just like his. I snap the book shut.

I grab a Coke and go over to the couch and click on the TV. *Terminator 2* is on the USA channel, which normally I would watch. I love the scene on the motorcycle. I love the way he can cock the shotgun with just one hand, and the sound it makes. Only I don't want to watch it with commercials. And *The Maltese Falcon* is on AMC, a classic. Another Dad favorite. I click around for a while, watching a little bit of *X-Treme Games* on ESPN and a cop show on NBC. And then *Aliens* starts on HBO.

"All right," I say out loud. I settle back, watching Ripley waking up from her cryo-sleep, watching her talk to the stupid guy from the company, the guy who wants to breed the aliens. What an idiot.

Only then I start remembering the time Dad and I rented all the *Alien* movies. "The entire canon," Dad said and laughed. Mom flipped out. She couldn't believe we were going to watch them all. Waste a whole day, she said. They're so violent and scary. They're so dumb, she said. And I remember Dad leaning over, putting his arm around her, and whispering, "Sigourney Weaver in her underwear, honey."

Only now I don't get it. Why would he say that? I mean,

did he *like* looking at Sigourney Weaver in her underwear. Or was he just pretending?

Ripley is still trying to figure out what the company guy is telling her.

But the really scary thought is, what if he wasn't pretending? What if he *liked* looking at girls in their underwear, and then, all of a sudden, he didn't. Is that how it works? One day you like girls. The next day you like guys.

The alien bulges up out of Ripley's chest. Mom is right. It's dumb. It's boring. I hate these movies. I click off the TV and go to bed.

By the time I get up in the morning, Mom and Grandma are already up. "Well, here he is!" Grandma says when I walk into the kitchen. She gives me a big hug and a kiss, which I wasn't expecting or I would have brushed my teeth. She steps back and looks at me. "He's the image of Steve at this age," she says to Mom over her shoulder. "Don't you think so, Marianne?"

Mom sets down her coffee cup. "I didn't actually know Steve when he was fifteen, Ruth." She gives me a little smile. "Ben always kind of reminds me of my brother. Especially when he laughs."

Grandma's shaking her head. "No. The image of Steve." She gives me another hug. She comes up to about my armpit. "How about some waffles?"

I look at the clock. It's eleven-thirty. I was thinking about having lunch. But I say, "Sure. Waffles sound great."

I sit down on the stool next to Mom and watch Grandma on the other side of the counter. She pulls a big bowl of batter out of the refrigerator and starts warming up the waffle iron. I didn't even know we owned a waffle iron. She talks nonstop, something about her neighbor in Redding and his nephew and how they're all going to take a bus trip to Branson, Missouri. I look at Mom. She hasn't put on her makeup yet, and she has dark circles under her eyes. She's tilting her coffee cup back and forth.

Grandma hands me a plate with a waffle the size of Rhode Island. She's covered it with peanut butter and bananas and a lake of maple syrup. "Real maple syrup," she says. "I brought it with me. Do you remember when you used to spend the weekend with Grandpa and me? I used to make you waffles like this."

I nod my head. My mouth is glued shut with peanut butter.

"Do you remember Grandpa, Ben?" Grandma leans on her elbows on the counter. "You were pretty young when he died." She looks at Mom. "Six or seven?"

"Seven," Mom says.

Grandpa had been big and bald and scary. He smoked, and when he'd lean down to talk to me, I could smell the cigarettes on him. I'd try to hold my breath. We'd learned about cigarettes in school, and I was always afraid I was going to die just smelling them on him.

"Do you remember him, Ben?" Grandma asks again as she sets a glass of orange juice down next to my plate.

"I remember him," I say. I take another bite of waffle. He used to take me out in the backyard to play catch with the football. He'd throw it just about as hard as he could. When I said it hurt my hands, he'd say . . .

"If it doesn't kill you, it'll make you stronger," Grandma says, smiling. "That's what he always said. He'd tell his players that."

"I'm sure that was very inspiring," Mom says. She's looking down into her coffee, like she's found something floating in it. "Your grandmother has a plan for the afternoon, Ben."

Good, I think. I have a plan, too. I'm going to the game with Sean and Chris. I take a big swig of juice. "What's your plan, Grandma?"

"I thought, wouldn't it be fun if you and your dad and I went to the football game this afternoon?"

I manage to put down the glass without spilling juice all over the place. I look at Mom. "Willamette View's game?" Mom is still staring at her coffee.

Grandma is nodding and smiling. "I haven't been to a game—oh, since Bud died, I suppose."

"The game this afternoon? That game?" I'm still looking at Mom.

"I talked to your father this morning," Grandma says. I look at her. She's still smiling. "He said he'd love to go. He said he'd pick us up at one. And I thought afterward we could go to Farrell's. I know how much you love their ice cream, Ben."

I haven't been to that restaurant since I was little. But I'm still trying to get my brain around Grandma and me and Dad. At the game. At the game with just about everybody I know in the entire world.

"I think Farrell's closed, Ruth," Mom says. "A couple of years ago."

Grandma stops smiling. She looks confused. "Well. We'll just have to find someplace else. Won't we, Ben?"

"But . . ."

She's wiping her hands on a dish towel. "I'm going to go

up and change right now. It looks like it might rain again."

When she's gone, I say, "Mom."

"I know. I know."

But I know she doesn't know. "I can't go to this football game with Grandma and Dad."

"Ben."

"But what about Chris and Sean? I promised I'd go with them."

"Tell them it's a family thing. I'm sure they'll understand." Mom sighs. "She just wants to do something with the two of you."

"Can't we just—I don't know—go to a movie or something?" A nice dark movie. Far away, in some other neighborhood.

Mom shakes her head. "She has this thing about going to the game. She's been going on and on about how wonderful it is that you're playing football now." Mom picks at a little blob stuck on the counter. "And I don't think she wants to be alone with your father. It turns out they've hardly spoken in the last few months. She thinks he's avoiding her."

I snort. "Yeah. I bet." But what if *I* don't want to be alone with *them*. Did anybody think of that? Did anybody think about good old Ben?

Mom stands up and carries my plate and her cup over to the sink. "Although Grandma was surprised. She said it was almost like your father knew she was in town."

"I told him," I say. And, right away, I know that was the wrong thing to say.

Mom turns around. "What? When?"

*I* pick at the blob. "Last night." I think about this. "He

was going to a movie," I say finally. "They've rereleased *Treasure of the Sierra Madre*."

"That sounds like your father." Mom leans back on the edge of the sink. "How was he?"

I shrug. "Okay, I guess. Keith was with him."

She folds her arms across her middle. "Really?" She takes in a deep breath, through her nose. "What's he like? Is he . . ." She looks like she's thinking about things Keith might be. "Young?" she says, finally.

"No. He's old. And bald." I remember him going on about Chynna needing permission to get pierced. "He was sort of a jerk." I suddenly have a terrible thought. "He's not coming is he? Today?"

"Oh, no." Mom laughs, although it doesn't sound like she thinks anything is funny. "I'm sure your father's not bringing Keith."

I groan. I put my head down on the counter. "I really, really don't want to do this."

I feel Mom's hand on my hair. "Oh, Ben. Remember. If it doesn't kill you . . ."

But it might, I think. It just might.

# Chapter
# Eleven

$D$ad shows up exactly at 1:00. He's driving a new black Audi.

Mom opens the door before he can ring the bell. "Hi, Steve," she says, like this is nothing different. Like he was just here yesterday. "Come on in."

"Hi, Marianne." He wipes his feet carefully and steps inside. He doesn't move any farther in. He just stands there on the little rug Mom keeps in front of the door. He's wearing the same jacket. The same highwater jeans. "Hi, Ben."

I get up from the couch. "Hey."

"Steve!" Grandma comes in from the kitchen. She's been scrubbing things. You can smell the disinfectant. "You look . . . It's so good to see you."

She crosses to him and hugs him, and he hugs her back. Sort of hugging and patting at the same time. "It's good to see you, too, Mom."

Grandma steps back. "Well." She's wiping her hands over and over on her apron. Mom never wears aprons. Grandma must have brought it with her. "Well," she says again.

"The house looks great, Marianne," Dad says. He nods toward the door. "And the yard."

"Ben's been mowing," Mom says.

They all look at me. Only Grandma looks normal. Mom and Dad look like aliens who've wandered onto the wrong planet. Coneheads. We're from France, I think. "It's not a big deal," I say. I *feel* like a Conehead.

Grandma says, "Mowing is . . ."

Dad says, "Well, I guess . . ."

And Mom says, "It should be . . ."

They all stop and laugh. "Go ahead, Mom," Dad says.

"Mowing is a big job with this yard," Grandma says. They all nod, seriously.

"Marianne?" Dad says. I think this must be the way he is in class, when he's calling on college students to answer history questions.

Mom laughs. "Oh. I was just going to say it should be a good game. Today."

Grandma claps her hands. "And we'd better hustle our bustles. You know what parking's like down by the stadium." She puts on her rain hat. "You'll need a jacket, Ben. It's probably going to rain."

Out on the driveway, I can tell that Grandma's thinking about sitting in the back. So I can sit up front with Dad. I push in front of her and flip the seat forward. "Let me sit in back, Grandma." I climb in.

"This is a nice car," Grandma says. "Is it new?"

"Uh-huh. I had to . . . Marianne and Ben have the Volvo." He glances back at me. "You have enough room there?"

"I'm fine," I say, but Grandma moves her seat forward, anyway. Her knees must be touching the dashboard.

"I don't think you have to go so far forward, Mom," Dad says.

"No, no. I know how long those legs are." She reaches back and tries to pat my knee, but she misses. "And you're living in Southeast?"

"Ladd's Addition. It's a nice, older neighborhood."

"In an apartment?"

"No. I'm sharing a house with a friend." Dad looks at me in the rearview mirror.

"Well. That's nice," Grandma says.

I don't say anything.

Grandma basically keeps up a running commentary all the way down to Civic Stadium. She goes on and on about the weather and how different it is in Redding and how much she likes Redding and what a good time she and her sister had on their bus trip to Las Vegas. Dad mumbles and nods, and every now and then checks on me in the mirror.

I haven't ridden in a car with Dad since I got my permit. It's sort of interesting to see how he drives. He accelerates like up to the very last possible moment. And he pulls in way too close to the cars in front of him. If the guy stopped all of a sudden, we'd be like toothpaste, squoodged right out of the tube. And he never signals. It's fun to make a list of his driving mistakes. He's not a very good driver.

We do have trouble finding a parking spot. By then, Grandma's run out of stories, and it's pretty quiet in the car. You can hear Dad swearing under his breath at loading zones and idiots who take up more than one space. I see an empty spot, about a block over, but I don't say anything.

I'm starting to hope maybe we'll just have to head back home.

Only then a car pulls out right in front of us.

"Perfect," Grandma says.

The stands are already filling up. As we make our way along the Willamette View section, looking for seats, we get stopped continually. There are lots of people who remember Grandma. And even more who remember Dad.

He keeps stopping to shake hands and slap shoulders. And he introduces me. "This is my son, Ben." He even introduces me to Mr. Yamaguchi, as if Chris and I haven't been playing together since football camp last June. As if Mr. Yamaguchi didn't drive me to half the games and practices. It makes me feel stupid.

But Mr. Yamaguchi just smiles and says, "Oh, I know Ben."

Grandma is talking to Mr. Hardesty, a vice principal. He's new at the school. I don't know how she knows him. And all I want is to sit down. Everybody in the entire section is watching. Watching Ben Gearhart and his crazy grandmother and his father.

Chris taps me on the shoulder. "Hey, Ben. We saved a seat for you. Me and Sean." He points up into the stands, and Sean and three other guys from the freshman team wave. They all have purple hair.

Dad turns around and sees Chris. "This is my son," Mr. Yamaguchi says.

Dad and Chris shake hands. I know Chris would die if he knew who he was shaking hands with. "I'm really glad to meet you, Mr. Gearhart. I have your number."

"My number?" Dad frowns.

"Well, I mean, not on the varsity team." Chris shrugs toward the field. "I'm just on the freshman team. But I'm Number Seven."

"Seven! A great number! A lucky number for me," Dad says.

"I told him," Mr.Yamaguchi says. "I told him it was a great number."

Grandma picks her way down the steps. She's been talking to a clump of old people halfway up in the stands. "We'd better sit down," she says. "It's going to start."

I look at Chris, and I'm going to say that I'm going to sit with him and the guys. But Dad grabs my arm. "I see three over there," he says.

We end up about four rows behind Sean and Chris. As soon as we sit down, Grandma hops back up. "I need a cup of coffee."

"I'll get it, Mom," Dad says.

"No. No. You know how I like to doctor it up. Do you boys want anything?"

Actually I'd love a burger and a Coke, but I say, "No, thanks," right after Dad.

As soon as she's gone, Dad leans back in his seat and sighs.

I don't know what he has to sigh about.

The field looks really nice. The grass is bright green, and the lines stand out straight and white.

"Too bad they have to mess it up," Dad says. He smiles at me, and it annoys me that he thinks I'm thinking what he's thinking.

There's a family a couple of rows below us, a mother and father with two little kids who look like they're in elementary school. "How come we never came to any of the games when I was little?"

He frowns. "I don't know. I never thought . . . Did you want to come to the games?"

I shrug. Maybe I had. I can't really remember. "Sure," I say. "It would have been fun."

He crosses his legs, uncrosses them. Crosses them the other way. "Were you and that girl going to the movie last night?"

I hate the way he says "that girl." I prop my feet up on the seat in front of me. "Chynna," I say. "Her name's Chynna. We *were* going to go to the movies, but we changed our minds."

He nods. He's looking at my sneakers. "I hope we didn't ruin your date. I mean, I hope you didn't change your plans because of Keith and me."

I can't believe he just said that out loud. I check behind me, to make sure no one back there heard him.

"Was that it, Ben?"

And I think, no, it didn't have anything to do with you. We weren't going to see a stupid black-and-white boring movie.

He clears his throat. "I know this must be . . . embarrassing for you, Ben."

I shut my eyes. I do not want to talk about this here, out in public, out in front of everybody.

"I wish we could talk about it some time."

This is the last thing in the world I would *ever* want to talk about, and I can't believe he doesn't know it.

But Grandma is coming back with a tray. She has coffee for herself and hot chocolate for me and Dad. It tastes good. "This is great, Grandma," I say. Dad nods. He has chocolate on his mustache. Grandma smiles and settles back in her seat.

The Wolverines score the first touchdown, and I forget all about Dad and Grandma.

At the half, the score is 14–13 for Willamette View. We all stand up as the team leaves the field. Grandma turns to Dad. "They need more defense, but, overall, they're not bad. Scrappy."

Dad smiles. "They're very scrappy. Aren't they, Ben?"

I'm watching John and Kyle. They're the last guys off the field. They've both taken off their helmets. Their faces are red, and their hair is dripping with sweat. John has his arm across Kyle's shoulders. I can imagine how they're feeling. Sore and tired and really pumped. The crowd roars even louder, and John and Kyle stop, like they've just noticed. They both grin and wave their helmets.

"I bet that brings back memories," Grandma says to Dad.

"Oh, yeah," Dad says.

We all sit down. Grandma leans across Dad toward me. "Steven just loved to play football. He lived for it."

Dad raises his eyebrows, but he doesn't say anything.

She smiles at him. "And it brought you so much closer to your father. You really forged some bonds." She puts her hand on his knee. "Do you remember that game against Beaverton? Your junior year? When the ref threw your father out?"

I laugh. I can imagine Grandpa ticking off some ref.

Dad smiles. "I remember."

"It was a great game. You boys just played your hearts out for him after that."

"We did," Dad says. He's staring down at the empty field.

"Did you win?" I ask.

He looks at me. "No. No, as a matter of fact, we lost. They kicked a field goal in the last ten seconds."

"It was a beautiful play," Grandma says.

"I thought I was going to die," Dad says.

"But you didn't," Grandma says. "You didn't. And it made you stronger. *And* brought you closer to your father."

Dad looks at her. People are moving up and down the steps. "Mom. It made me crazy. I didn't come out of my room for two days."

Grandma shakes her head. "I don't remember *that*. But I do remember it was a great game." She looks at me. "Are you hungry, Ben? Do you want a hot dog or something?"

I shake my head.

Dad is leaning toward Grandma. "You know what drives me crazy, Mom? The way you are continually rewriting history."

"I don't know what you're talking about, Steven."

"You only see things the way you want to. Like Karen's first marriage? And . . ."

I stand up, fast. "You know, I am going to get something to eat." I don't wait for them to say anything. I turn around and go out the other way, stepping over a bunch of people near the aisle. When I get to the bottom of the steps, I look back up. Grandma is sitting with her arms folded and her eyes shut. Dad is still leaning toward her, talking. I'm really glad to see that all the seats around them are empty.

Chris and his dad are standing in line at the snack bar. "Good game, huh?" Chris says.

"It must really be bringing back some old feelings for your dad," Mr. Yamaguchi says.

"Oh, yeah," I say. I think about asking them if they could give me a ride home, but I can't think of a good reason.

I hang out in the snack area as long as I can. Finally, when I've eaten all the ice out of my cup, and when the band has filed off the field, I head back toward my seat. But Dad is standing, leaning against the railing at the foot of the stairs.

"Your grandmother's out in the car," he says. He's scanning the faces in the stands. Not looking at me.

I want to tell him that I want to stay for the rest of the game. I want to tell him that I can get a ride home. I want to tell him that I don't want to ride home in that car with them.

There's a roar as the Wolverines come back out on the field.

Dad looks down at me. He has tears in his eyes.

Oh, God. I turn toward the exit. "Let's go."

# Chapter
## Twelve

Grandma doesn't say a single word in the car all the way home. She just sits there in the back seat, staring straight ahead. I can see her in the little rearview mirror on my side of the car. She doesn't even have her seat belt on. But I don't mention it.

I keep waiting for Dad to say something, to try to make her feel better. He's supposed to be good at that kind of thing. In movies, they're always way more sensitive than the straight guys. They dress better. They live in nicer apartments. And they always know what to say when somebody's upset. I mean, you'd think that, out of all this crap, at least we'd get somebody who could talk about his feelings.

But Dad doesn't say anything the whole ride home either.

Finally we pull into our driveway. I climb out of the car and let Grandma out of the back seat. She doesn't say a word. She just walks past me and on into the house.

Dad is still sitting in the car, not moving. He looks worse than he did when he told Mom and me.

Back in May, he'd said, "I just hope that someday, Ben, you'll be able to understand."

Like I don't understand right now.

I lean my head back into the car. "You could get AIDS, you know."

He turns toward me. He blinks, and his mouth hangs open, like his bottom lip has suddenly gotten too heavy to hold up. "I . . ." He clears his throat. "I'm in a monogamous relationship. And Keith and I have both been . . ."

I put my hand up. Stop, stop. "But did you know in high school?"

"What?" He blinks again. "About AIDS?"

I can't believe he's this dense. I take a deep breath. "You definitely knew that you liked guys," I say slowly. "Back in high school. You knew then?"

"I definitely knew in high school, Ben. In fact, I knew even before then." He reaches out a hand, like he's going to touch me, only he lets it fall on the passenger seat.

"So what about Sigourney Weaver?"

"Sigourney Weaver?" He says it like it's a trick question. "What about her?"

I can't see explaining all of this in the middle of the driveway. "Never mind." I straighten up. Then I lean back down. "Grandma's just really old, you know."

He nods. "I know that."

"She doesn't expect stuff like this."

He nods again.

I stand back up. He leans forward, so he can see me.

"Ben . . ." He looks at me, then shakes his head. "Just let me know how the game turned out, okay? Call me."

"Right." I slap the roof of the car, once. Then I go up the steps. The car is out of the driveway before I get in the house. Grandma is standing in the living room. She still has her coat on and her little plastic rain hat. She's staring down at her shoes. Mom is standing in the kitchen doorway. "Ruth? Are you sure you're all right?" she says. She looks at me, her eyebrows raised.

"I am so glad Bud is dead," Grandma says. "Because this would kill him." She looks at Mom. "I think I'll lie down for a while, Marianne." She walks off down the hall. She walks like a little old lady.

When her door shuts, Mom looks at me. "He told her at the football game?"

"At halftime. I was getting a Coke."

"That was probably not the best time," she says slowly.

"Yeah. Not real sensitive." I think about the ratty old jacket. The high-water pants. He can't get anything right. "He doesn't even dress any better."

Mom frowns. "What?"

"Never mind." I go off to my room, too. I put my headphones on and turn up the volume on the Discman. Really loud.

The next morning Mom announces that we're going to church. We almost never go to church. I hate having to get up early on a Sunday. I hate having to get dressed up. But she says, "It's a chance for Grandma to see old friends. It'll make her happy." Maybe it does, but Grandma doesn't act much happier.

After the service, Grandma is talking to some old couple

she used to know when she lived here before. Mom pulls me to one side.

"Listen. I've asked her to stay a little while longer with us. I don't think she should go home when she's so upset. I think she needs some time to . . . adjust."

I think she's going to need a lot more than time, but I just say, "Okay."

After lunch, Mom and Grandma take off for the grocery store. I call Jeremy. I have to find out what happened at the game. I don't want to look like a total fool on Monday. "Hey. Were you at the game yesterday?"

"Yeah. Weren't you? I thought I saw you."

"It's a long story. So who won?"

"They did. Kicked a field goal in the last thirty seconds."

"You're kidding!"

"Nope. It totally sucked. Hey. Guess what?"

"What?"

"Angie dumped the roller-hockey guy."

"Oh. Right. Great. So, you wearing the bracelet again?"

He laughs. "Maybe. I didn't throw it away." He hangs up. I think about calling Dad, but I don't.

When Mom and Grandma get home, I help them unload the groceries and put them away. "Willamette View lost yesterday. Barlow kicked a field goal in the last thirty seconds."

Grandma looks at me.

"That's too bad," Mom says. She's trying to jam two packages of chicken and a ham into the refrigerator. "So they're out of the playoffs?"

"Yeah." I'm kneeling down, stacking cans in the pantry. "I bet the defense feels really bad. And the quarterback. Kyle. I'll bet he feels awful."

104

Grandma doesn't say anything. She just hands me some boxes of macaroni and cheese. "Put these in there, too."

All the posters are still up at school on Monday. "Whomp 'em Wolverines!" and "Blast Barlow!" I see Kyle at his locker. So he's not staying in his room. Not like Dad. In algebra, when Mr. Venner asks them what happened on Saturday, Kyle says, "The defense screwed up." John gets him in a headlock, and they wrestle around. They knock over two desks before Mr. Venner finally gets them to stop. John stands on his chair and shouts, "Wait till next year!" Everybody laughs. But when they finally sit down, Kyle isn't smiling. And when Chynna tries to get his attention, he ignores her. I remember how much he wanted to add another trophy to the case in the commons. Chynna raises her eyebrows at me. I shrug.

Grandma makes chicken and dumplings on Monday night. She makes pot roast and mashed potatoes on Tuesday night. She makes stew on Wednesday. We eat all the meals in the dining room. Grandma puts knives and forks and spoons at every place, whether we need them or not. She folds the napkins. It reminds me of one of those old sitcoms they show on *Nick at Nite*. We have the food and the plates and the silverware. Now all we need is the family to go with it.

Kyle and John cut algebra on Tuesday and Wednesday, and I'm sort of glad. And I take the back way into the cafeteria. I don't want to end up sitting with the varsity team. I don't know what to say to them. Tough game? Good try? Everything I think of sounds really stupid. I eat lunch with Chris and Sean.

On Thursday I cut through the Latino hall on my way to

the cafeteria. Back in September, Jeremy called it the scary Mexican hall. Kids are standing around in clumps, talking Spanish. It always sounds like they're yelling at each other. We don't learn this stuff in Spanish class. I know Kyle and John and the other guys don't go this way much either.

Officer Wilkins is coming down the hall with Chad the drug-sniffing dog. Chad and Officer Wilkins spend a lot of time in the Latino hall and in the African-American hall. You never see them around the computer lab or the locker rooms. You never see them under the bleachers.

Chad is mostly sniffing wrappers and stuff on the floor. Kids are patting him. I stop to scratch his ears. "Hey, Chad. How's it going?" He thumps his tail against a locker.

A classroom door opens, and John and Kyle come out. "Hey, Chad!" John shouts. "Good old Chad!" He wraps his arms around the dog and gives him a big hug.

"Please do not hug the dog," Officer Wilkins says. "You may pat him or scratch his ears, but please don't hug him."

"That's right, John, you pervert. No huggin' the freakin' dog," Kyle says, and the kids around us all laugh. He looks at me. "Hey, Ben. You going to lunch?"

"I . . . well . . . yeah."

"Come on then. Let's go."

We take up almost all the hallway, Kyle and John and me, and groups of kids have to break up and go around us. Walking with them, I feel really big, but good big.

"Manly men," Kyle says, like he knows exactly what I'm thinking.

I laugh. "Tough game," I say, after a minute.

John snorts. Kyle shrugs.

In the cafeteria, John and Kyle push to the head of the

line and grab pizza. We all sit down at a table with Patterson and Drucker and two girls I don't know.

As soon as we sit down, Patterson mumbles something. He gets up and leaves.

"What's his problem?" John asks.

One of the girls raises her eyebrows. "He's still bummed out about that game."

"Get over it," John says. "There's always next year."

"Patterson's a senior, idiot," Kyle says.

"Oh. That's right." For just a second, John looks embarrassed. I've never seen John Maybry look like that. "Well. Maybe he can play in college," John says.

Drucker and Kyle exchange looks. "I don't think he's good enough," Drucker says, finally. "I mean, he's a nice guy . . ."

The three of them just sit there. They don't even eat. The girls look at each other. One of them makes a little face. Across the room, I see Sean and Chris and a bunch of guys from the freshman team. They're throwing around a big wad of foil, laughing like maniacs.

"If it doesn't kill you, it'll make you stronger," I say.

John and Drucker look at *me*, which is maybe worse than having them staring at their pizza.

"What?" Kyle says.

I shrug. I know I'm blushing. "It's this thing my grandmother says. This dumb thing."

"It's true, though," John says. "It will make you stronger. I like that." Kyle and Drucker both nod. They're smiling. John reaches over and punches me, hard. "I like you, little guy." He takes a big bite of his pizza.

Kyle watches me pull sandwiches and cookies out of my

bag. Grandma made me lunch. "Chynna told me she asked you to the party. At Weiker's."

Drucker looks over at us, but he doesn't say anything.

I unwrap a sandwich. "Yeah. She said something about it."

"It's going to be a great party. Todd's family's out of town."

"You should come, man," John says suddenly. "It'll be good for you."

Drucker laughs, but he nods. He puts his arm around one of the girls. She laughs, too.

"I can pick you up," Kyle says. "Give you a ride if you need one." He leans forward and says, quietly, "I'd really appreciate it if you'd come, Ben."

I don't know why it matters to him. Does he need a bodyguard, too? But John and Drucker are looking at me. The two girls are looking at me. "Sure," I say. "Sounds good."

I spend the rest of the day trying to figure out how I'm going to convince Mom it sounds good.

I bring it up at dinner—ham and scalloped potatoes. "Tomorrow night," I say. "There's this party."

Before Mom can say anything, Grandma says, "A party! Wonderful!" She looks at Mom. "He needs to get out of the house, be with people his own age." Like I don't go to school all day. "He spends way too much time in front of that TV."

"I didn't say he has to stay home, Ruth." Mom looks at me. "A party. Where?"

"Todd Weiker's. He's on the varsity team."

"The varsity team," Grandma says. She waves her fork at

me. It has a piece of ham stuck on the end. "It's good for you to get to know them. To get the feel of the team."

I'm not sure that's what I'm supposed to get the feel of, but I don't say anything.

"So the football team is having a party," Mom says. She turns a little toward me, like she's trying to concentrate, trying to tune Grandma out. "Tomorrow night."

"Yeah," I say. I figure I'll go for her sympathetic side. "It was supposed to be a celebration, I think. But then, you know, they lost." I make a sad face.

"They need to get together to support each other," Grandma says. "After a game like the one on Saturday. Your grandfather always said it's as important to mourn your defeats as it is to celebrate your victories."

"Bud said *that?*" Mom asks.

"Of course, he always told his teams that if they had any defeats to mourn, he'd kick their butts from here to Christmas." Grandma gives a little cackle, and she looks like the old Grandma. Just for a second.

Mom laughs. "That sounds like Bud." She looks at me. "How will you get to this party? I've got a dinner thing with the company, and your grandmother won't be here."

"You got a date, Grandma?" I ask.

She doesn't smile. "Friends from the church. They asked me over for dinner."

I nod. Do her good to get out of the house. Be around people her own age. "Kyle said he'd give me a ride. Kyle Cameron."

"The quarterback," Grandma says. "You can always trust the quarterback to be smart and sensible, Marianne." She leans forward and puts her hand over Mom's. "You know. Maybe if Steve had gotten out more in high school. Had more fun . . ."

Mom puts her other hand over Grandma's. They look like they're going to play that game where you pile your hands up and the hand on the bottom moves up to the top. "I think it would be fine for Ben to go to the party, Ruth." She looks at me. "Because I know *he's* smart and sensible."

Smart and sensible. It sounds like a curse. But I just nod and smile.

# Chapter
## Thirteen

Grandma is already gone when I get home from school on Friday. When Mom gets home she says, "Let's order a pizza." We eat at the kitchen counter. Pizza out of the box. Diet Coke out of the can.

"I thought you were going out for dinner," I say.

"I'm just having one slice." She sighs. "This is good. When is Kyle picking you up?"

"Eight."

"And when will you be home?"

I pick a piece of pepperoni off and eat it. "I'm not really sure. It's a party, Mom."

"We need to settle on a time, Benjamin. I don't want to be calling the cops at two-thirty in the morning."

I don't want that either. "One-thirty," I say.

"Ha!" She laughs once, loud and sharp, like the teacher on *The Simpsons*. "No way, buddy. You're fifteen years old." Like that has anything to do with anything. "Eleven," she says.

"Eleven! Mom. Come on." I give her my "I can't believe you're serious" look.

"Eleven-thirty," she says.

"Twelve-thirty."

"Midnight." She holds up her hand. "That's it, Ben. No more negotiation. Midnight or nothing."

"Okay, okay." Actually, I'm pretty happy. Midnight's not too bad. I can see myself telling people I have to be home by midnight. My mother, I'll say. And I'll roll my eyes.

The doorbell rings. "That's Linda picking me up," Mom says. She scoops up her purse and jacket. "I'm not sure when I'll be home. We might go out afterward. But Grandma will be back in time to check on you." She kisses me on the top of my head. "Have a good time," she says.

"Okay."

I turn on the TV. The movies all suck, so I click through the commercial channels. Mostly sitcoms and a really awful lawyer show.

I know there's going to be booze at the party. Definitely beer, because just about everybody on the team drinks it. Other stuff, depending on what Todd's dad keeps around the house. Pot, for sure.

I figure I'll drink beer. Budweiser, if they have it. I like their commercials. The ones with the iguanas or the chameleons or whatever they are. I don't know about the drugs. I've never smoked anything or snorted anything. I don't want to look like a total fool. What if I get this big coughing fit? Or I exhale instead of inhale? I saw a movie where that happened. The cocaine went all over the place. Beer is safer. I already know how to drink stuff.

Thinking about it, I get up and grab another Coke from the fridge. I stand there with the door open, looking at all the leftovers Grandma's stored away in Tupperware bowls. I didn't even know we owned that much Tupperware.

And then there's sex. This might be my chance. Not to start counting. Not like John and Kyle. But just a chance.

"In your dreams, Gearbutt," I say out loud to the leftovers. I shut the door and take my Coke back to the couch.

Kyle and Chynna finally show up after eight. I've checked my deodorant three times. Changed my shirt twice.

I go out on the porch as soon as I hear the car. Only it's the Mapes's Honda sitting in the driveway. I stop, my hand on the doorknob. Then I see Kyle behind the wheel. He lifts one hand, waves. Chynna leans out of the passenger window. "Come on, Ben. We're *late.*"

Like that's my fault.

I climb in the back.

Kyle turns and looks at me. "Hey, hog. How's it going?"

"Okay."

Chynna grins back at me, too. "You have enough room? I can move the seat forward." She's wearing the leather jacket again. She doesn't look like she's worrying about Kyle or anything else.

"I'm fine," I say.

Kyle backs out of the driveway. He uses all the rearview mirrors, and he looks over his shoulder. His truck is parked by the curb in front of Chynna's house, a red Toyota. He nods out the window at it. "My truck died. I can't believe it. I don't know what's wrong with it."

"And your parents let us use their car?" I ask the back of Chynna's head.

"They aren't exactly actually home," she says. She's

looking out at the dark house. "I found the spare keys. But I know they wouldn't mind. They love Kyle."

Kyle laughs and shakes his head.

"The first time they met him, he shook my dad's hand and said, 'I'm glad to meet you, Mr. Mapes.'" She makes her voice low and deep, and Kyle and I both laugh.

"I'm such a suck-up," Kyle says. He laughs again. He points at the truck. "Damn. I hope it's not the alternator."

"Maybe it's just the battery," I say. "Maybe you just need a jump."

"You got any cables?"

"I don't think so."

"Maybe in your trunk?" He turns back around to look at me.

I don't have a set of keys to Mom's car. And there aren't any spare keys. "I think my dad took the jumper cables. When he moved out."

"We could check."

"Guys," Chynna says. "We are already so late."

"Okay." Kyle turns back around. "Maybe later."

At the corner, he stops at the stop sign and turns on the radio. Old sixties music floods the car. "Change it!" Chynna shrieks. "Change it quick!"

Kyle fiddles with the buttons and finds an alternative rock station. "Aaah." He lets out a big sigh. I give him a thumbs-up in the rearview mirror. Kyle cranks up the bass. Very nice system, Mrs. Mapes. We pull out onto Sherman.

The speakers are right behind my head, and the bass is really thumping. I can feel it in my teeth. I lean forward, just a little.

Chynna is hanging on to Kyle's right arm. She has her

**114**

seat belt on, and she has to lean against it. It doesn't look real comfortable. Kyle's tapping his hand on the steering wheel, humming to the music. He's a good driver, though, real smooth.

He looks in the rearview mirror at me. "Gonna have a great time tonight, Ben." He has to shout a little, above the music. He looks happy. Happier than I've seen him all week.

I nod. "You bet."

"You have a curfew or anything?"

"Well. I probably need to be back around midnight." Now it sounds way too early. "Or twelve-thirty." I'll work it out with Mom after it happens.

Chynna's head jerks up. "Twelve-thirty?"

But Kyle is nodding. "That's cool," he says.

We stop at the red light on Pacific Highway. Kyle's trying to turn right, but there's a lot of traffic.

A tan Aerostar pulls into the lane beside us. A man and a woman are sitting in the front, two little kids in the back. The woman looks out her window at us.

All of a sudden, I know I must look pretty stupid. There's Kyle and Chynna, up front, obviously a couple. And what am I doing, sitting there all alone in the back seat. Like a little kid.

Kyle pulls out. I lean back, try to scrunch myself down into the corner. The speaker blares into my ear. I'm getting a headache.

We go a long ways on Pacific Highway. Out where there are no more streetlights. Out where the speed limit increases to fifty-five.

"Where in the hell are we going?" Chynna asks.

Kyle digs in his pocket and pulls out a piece of paper. "We're going to Todd's dad's girlfriend's place. That's where they're all living now, I guess. But his dad and the girlfriend are in Hawaii. These are the directions."

"These are streets?" Chynna asks.

"Don't worry, hon," Kyle says. And he leans over and kisses her.

I really don't know why I've come along.

We make a left off Pacific Highway, onto a little road. We almost miss the turn. We pass lots of empty fields. A few houses. A sign that says LLAMA RANCH.

The next street we turn on is even smaller and darker. Only a little country road. We pass two houses, close together, and then open fields. In the moonlight, I see a barn in one field, maybe some cows in another. Kyle slows down, looking for mailboxes.

Only it's not like we can miss the house. It's a big white house, set a little back from the road. A nice house. It sort of reminds me of the one at the end of *Scream*. There are cars all over, filling the driveway, on the grass, parked along the street. The house blazes up above them. It looks like every light is on.

Kyle pulls into the gravel driveway and parks on the grass next to Mike Evans's red and yellow Gran Torino. Kyle turns off the engine. My ears ring in the sudden silence. The front door of the house opens, and Todd steps out on the porch. Pure noise pours out with him. Music, laughter, yelling. We can hear it inside the car with the windows rolled up.

"Hey, hog!" Todd shouts. "About time you got here!"

We all climb out. Kyle opens the trunk. He pulls out two

twelve packs of beer. He hands one to me. "Your contribution," he says, grinning.

"Thanks." It's Budweiser.

I follow Kyle and Chynna up the steps. Todd is standing at the top. He's swaying a little. I can't tell if it's to the music or just because he's swaying. Kyle puts his hand flat on his chest and pushes Todd back from the steps. Todd grins. "Welcome to the party."

Inside, it really stinks. Sweat, perfume, cigarette smoke, pot. The living room is packed with people. Music is blaring out of a CD player. It's the same CD Chris lent me. Kids are kind of milling around. Two couples are making out at opposite ends of a long leather couch.

We throw our jackets in a big pile that's falling out of the front hall closet.

"This way. Watch out. Coming through." Todd shoves his way across the room, holding Kyle's case of beer on his head like a native bearer in an old Tarzan movie. Chynna has a tight grip on Kyle's arm. Like she's afraid she'll lose him.

Patterson pushes past us. "Hey, man!" Kyle gives him a high five. "Glad you could make it."

"Having a great time," Patterson says, and he laughs.

There are two guys and some girls sitting around a big wooden table in the kitchen. One of the guys is rolling joints from a plastic bag in the middle of the table.

Todd points to three coolers set up by the stove. "Beer and wine in here." He grabs a beer and pops the top. Some of it spills down his shirt, but he doesn't notice. "Pool table and stuff downstairs. Bedrooms upstairs, but they're pretty much occupied at the moment." Chynna giggles, but Kyle just shrugs. "Oh. But no hot tub," Todd adds. "Something's wrong with the filter."

"That sucks," Kyle says.

"Sorry, man."

"Hey, Todd." A girl comes in from the living room. "You're out of toilet paper and salsa and somebody broke the . . . the— Ooh. Pot." She sits down at the table.

"Oh, hell." Todd grabs another beer and heads off into the living room. "Don't trash my house!" he roars.

One of the girls holds a joint out to Kyle. "Want a hit?"

Chynna looks like she's going to grab it, but Kyle says, "Later, hon."

Chynna looks ticked. "Well. At least I'm going to have a beer." She opens the nearest cooler and grabs a Coors. She opens it and drinks the whole thing while Kyle and I kind of stand there, staring. She wipes her mouth. "Want one, Ben?"

"Uh. No. I'll have one of these." I'm still carrying the Bud.

"Those are warm," Kyle says. "Have a cold one." Chynna's started on another one.

"Naw. That's okay. I like Bud." I set the case on the floor, open it up and grab a can. It's bigger than I expected, taller than a Coke. I pop the top and take a swig.

One time, when I was like seven, I drank a glass of pickle juice because Jeff Austin dared me to. The warm Bud is almost as bad. Not quite, but real close. I manage to swallow it, and I turn around, hoping Chynna and Kyle aren't standing there, laughing at me.

Only Chynna and Kyle have disappeared.

The girl who was worried about the toilet paper and salsa looks up at me. "Lose something?"

"Uh. No. Not really."

She holds out the joint. It's smoldering gently. "Want some?"

I hold up the can of beer. "Think I'll finish this first."

"Wouldn't want to mix your Bud and your bud," one of the guys says, and they all start laughing.

I go into the living room. I check my watch. It's a long time till midnight.

# Chapter
# Fourteen

I edge myself around the pack of people in the living room. I try to find somebody I know, somebody I can hang with for a while.

The bodies in front of me part for a second, and I see Chynna and Kyle across the room. Kyle's talking to Brad, the punt kicker. Chynna has one hand up the back of Kyle's shirt. She has a wine cooler in the other hand. I wonder if she really finished the second beer that fast. She looks pretty happy, though. Not like she needs a bodyguard.

Someone has put a Daddies CD on the player. "We're skankin'!" Rivas shouts, and a bunch of kids start dancing.

Three girls sit down next to my feet. "So then, she tells him that I said . . ." The girl stops and looks up at me. "Do you mind? This is sort of a private conversation."

"Oh. Sure." I step over two of the girls and start working my way around the room. Rivas spins a girl, and I just manage to dodge her. I push over to the coffee table. I grab a handful of chips out of a bowl.

Patterson is dancing with Tiffani, one of the cheerleaders. And I see Amber Parks, in a corner, talking to Drucker. She's laughing, her hand on his chest. Amber Parks? The crowd shifts, and she disappears. I can't see Kyle and Chynna anywhere.

I move out of the living room and back into the front hall. The door is open, and cold air is blowing into the house. It feels really good. I lean against the edge of the door and eat the chips.

Kids are out on the porch, leaning on the railing. They're watching two guys out on the lawn punching each other. Nobody says anything, not the people on the porch, not the two guys. You can hear grunting and the sound of fists hitting bodies.

I turn around. John is coming down the stairs. He has his arm around a girl from my Spanish class. Courtney, I think.

"Hey, Gearbutt!" John shouts at the top of his lungs. "How's it hangin'? Havin' fun?"

I hold up the beer can. "Havin' fun."

Courtney wiggles out from under his arm. "I'm going to get a beer." She pushes into the living room.

"Get one for me!" John shouts. He leans toward me. His eyes are bloodshot. He smells of beer and cigarette smoke and something else. Sweat, I think. "I am having a very, very good time, Benny boy. A very, very, good time." He takes something out of his pocket and presses it into my hand.

It's a condom.

"You can have one," he says. "I have lots." He leans toward me even farther. "It's now or never, Ben."

"Thanks, John." I shove the condom into my pocket. I

start to move past him. I'm afraid he's going to fall on me. "I gotta go."

"Bathrooms all over the place!" John waves his arms. "Whole house full of bathrooms!" He spots the open door. "All right! Fight!" he yells, even louder than before.

The first room down the hall *is* a bathroom. The door is open. There are a bunch of girls standing in front of the mirror, messing with their hair. They look at me as I pass by, then they laugh.

The next door is a closet. A girl says, "Go away!" And a guy laughs. I shut the door.

The hall opens up at the end to a big room, an office of some kind. There's a desk along one wall, and six guys are huddled around a computer screen. One of them says, "Watch out for the trapdoor." And another says, "Shoot him! Shoot him!"

They're playing really loud rap music on a CD player on a shelf. I hate rap music. I can feel the condom wrapper digging into my leg. I think about Monday morning. I think about John and Patterson and Drucker and Kyle counting. Adding up. Asking me how I did Saturday night. I take another sip of the beer. It still tastes bad.

One of the guys looks at me. "You want to sit down?"

"No. That's okay." I'm not going to spend the whole night in the nerd room. "I was just leaving."

The closet door is open. The bathroom door is shut. Three girls are lined up next to it, their arms folded across their chests. "We're next," they all say at the same time.

Kyle and Chynna come out of the living room as I step back into the front hall. Chynna has another beer. Her face is flushed. She's laughing.

"Hey, Ben," Kyle says. He looks glad to see me.

"Having a great time," I say, before he can ask. I check my watch. After nine. "You know. I have to be home . . ."

"Not until twelve-thirty." Chynna squints at me. Her eyes are a little bloodshot. Then, suddenly, she puts her hand on my arm. "I am having a really good time, Ben."

"Great," I say.

"Of course you're having a good time," Kyle says. He's looking past me, out the front door.

Chynna takes a big swig of beer. Then she stretches up toward Kyle's ear, whispers something.

Kyle looks at me. "So. You're good, Ben?"

"Yeah. Great." Chynna's hand is in his shirt again. Maybe in the waistband of his jeans. "I was thinking about playing some pool. It's downstairs?"

Kyle nods. He takes a step closer to Chynna. "Door's in the kitchen," he says. "To the basement."

The air in the kitchen is heavy with smoke. Kids are still sitting at the table, but no one is talking. They're just sort of leaning back, staring off into space. Two girls are microwaving popcorn. One of them leans, briefly, against my chest. "I have the munchies so bad," she murmurs. Her forehead leaves a wet spot on my shirt.

It smells like the popcorn is burning.

I finally find the door to the basement. It's cooler on the stairs. Cooler and quieter. I pull the door shut behind me.

There's a big room at the bottom of the stairs. Kids are clustered around a pool table. As I walk in, one of them puts the cue ball in and they laugh. Someone has knocked over a can of beer, and it's puddling on the floor.

It's the kind of basement that's not really underground.

At the far end of the room, big sliding glass doors open to the backyard. Five guys are sitting around a table in front of the doors, playing poker. They're all smoking cigars. They have a bottle of scotch and short, thick glasses with ice and booze in them. There's a hundred-dollar bill on the top of the pile of money in the middle of the table.

I stand there, watching the pool game, fingering the condom in my pocket. No virgins on varsity. Now or never. It'll make you stronger.

There's a loud burst of laughter behind a door to my right. I open the door. The only light is from a TV in the corner. Kids are jammed onto a long couch and a couple of chairs and the floor. It looks pretty crowded, and I'm backing out, when someone says, "Ben!"

The screen flickers, brightens, and I see Megan Frasier. She scoots over in her chair. "Come and sit down. We're watching *South Park*."

There's not a whole lot of room in the chair, but I squish down in between her and the arm.

"I'm glad to see you," she says.

"Oh, wow. Me, too," I say.

"Todd has all the *South Park* episodes recorded," she whispers.

"Shh!" a kid on the floor says.

Megan leans closer to me. "This is the *bris* episode. It's a Jewish ceremony . . ."

"I know what it is," I say. "I've seen this one."

"Shh!" the kid says again.

Megan and I look at each other, and we both laugh. I settle back against the cushion. I can feel her leg and her arm and her side, all pressed up against me. I put the beer down on the floor. The kid drinks it.

We watch all of the *bris* episode and the Christmas episode, too. When it's over, Megan sighs. "I like that one because Kenny doesn't die."

"Yeah. Me, too."

She stands up. "I need something to drink."

I get up and follow her. Two kids leap into our chair as soon as we're gone.

The pool game is still going on. There's a big pile of money in front of the poker players. Megan points to the sliding door. "Let's go outside. It's so smoky in here."

There's a patio outside the doors, with a big plastic table and lots of chairs scattered around. Behind them is the hot tub. The only light comes from inside the house. No one is out here. It's cold after the inside, but not a bad cold.

Megan is bending over a cooler shoved up against the wall. She's wearing a short skirt and black tights. You can see all the muscles in her legs. Soccer player legs. Great quads. She straightens up and hands me a can. "Want one?"

I've already decided I'm going to drink it, no matter what. Maybe this will all be easier if I'm drunk. Now or never. But she's handed me a diet Coke. "Oh, hey." I drink half of it in one gulp.

Megan sits down on one of the chaise lounges. She leans back. "Laurel and I hid a stash out here. Laurel Morgan? Do you know her?"

I sit down in the chair next to her. "Yeah, sure."

Megan takes a sip of Coke. "She's helped me out so

much on the team this year. But I guess it's like that on the football team, too, huh?"

"Like what?"

"You know. The older guys sort of show you the ropes. Give you advice."

"Oh, yeah." Advice and condoms. I finish the Coke. Clear my throat. "I'm not actually on the varsity team, you know."

"You will be, though. We used to watch the freshmen play. Because your games were at the same time as practice."

"The soccer team watched us play?" I am so glad I didn't know this at the time. I sit back in the chair.

"Well, usually not the whole game. But Laurel said you had great speed and natural agility. She said you could probably play soccer even, if you wanted to."

I can tell this is supposed to be a compliment. "I need to work on my speed," I say.

She sighs. "Tell me about it. I feel like I spend half my time just chasing faster players. I don't even get my foot on the ball."

I nod. "At least they don't knock you down and step on you."

"That must really suck," she says. She laughs. And I'm thinking how nice she is and how much I like her. And I realize I like her so much, I can't even imagine saying the word "condom" to her. Or anything else like that.

The sound from upstairs has been sort of a dull roar behind us, but now it rises, suddenly. There's a crash, followed by silence, and then a whole lot of laughter.

"You come to a lot of these parties?" Megan asks.

"First one."

"Me, too. And I'm just here because Laurel asked me to come along. So she could see Kyle."

I'm still thinking about how much I like her. "Kyle? Kyle Cameron?"

"There's another Kyle on the planet?" Megan sips her Coke. "Ever since they broke up, Laurel's been *baaad.*" She draws out the word, shaking her head. "So when Kyle called her . . ."

"Kyle called Laurel?"

"Well, she called him first. You know. When they lost the game. And then he called her back and said he really wanted to see her, and he really, really missed her. And he told her about this party."

I'm still trying to get this into my brain. "Kyle told Laurel to come to this party?"

Megan sits back in her chair. She's almost completely in darkness. "It's actually sort of nice, you know. They have this agreement thing. Kyle and Laurel. They've promised to save themselves for each other."

I laugh. I can't help it. "Oh, yeah. Right."

Megan shakes her head. "Laurel told me all about it. They think they have a really special relationship, and sex would ruin it." I can't see her face very well. "And Kyle told her on the phone he hasn't slept with anybody. Since they broke up. He's still a virgin." She leans forward, gives me a serious look. "This is a total secret."

I feel like I've clicked into the middle of some really complicated movie. Like the first time I saw *Pulp Fiction.* "Kyle Cameron?" I say, slowly and clearly.

Megan frowns. "There's another Kyle on the planet?"

She snaps her fingers. "Wait a minute. We're back where we started." She reaches over and puts her hand on my leg. "Ooh," she says. "Nice quads." She grins. "Maybe we could work out together some time. You could spot me."

I grin. "Sure. Sounds—"

The sliding door rattles open. Chynna is standing there, silhouetted by the light. She's crying. "I want to go home," she says. "I want to go home right now."

# Chapter
## Fifteen

W hat?"

Chynna wipes the back of her hand across her eyes, like a little kid. It smears her mascara all over the place. "I need you to drive me home, Ben." She holds up her other hand and jingles a set of car keys.

I look at Megan. She shrugs. "Maybe I should leave you two alone." And before I can stop her, she's gone, past Chynna, through the door.

Chynna steps aside to let Megan by. She stumbles, nearly trips and finally sits down, heavily, on the cooler. She bends her head down onto her knees and starts crying again, really loud.

The poker players are all staring at us. I get up and close the door. "What happened?"

She looks up at me. Her nose is running. Strands of hair are plastered to the sides of her cheeks. Her makeup has made a raccoon mask around her eyes. "Do you know who Kyle is with right now?"

"Laurel Morgan?"

She gives a big, ugly snort. "How did you know? Does everybody know?"

"I just guessed."

Chynna takes a deep, shaky breath. "He said he really needs to spend time with Laurel. He asked me if I could find someone to drive me home." Her eyes are filling up. She puts her head back down and starts sobbing again, even louder than before.

I look at the guys playing poker. One of them smiles at me and shakes his head. Like this is my fault. Like I'm the one who made her cry. I don't even want to be out here. I want to find Megan. I want to sit and talk to Megan. My head is starting to ache again.

Chynna tips her head back. "Kyle Cameron, I hate your guts!" She drops her head back down.

"Shh," I say. "Shh." I pat her, gently, on the top of the head.

"I want to go home," she moans. She looks up at me. "Please, Ben. You promised you'd help me. Please take me home."

"Okay," I say. "Okay. Let me think." Obviously I can't ask Kyle. I could ask John, but he's drunk. In fact, just about everybody here is drunk. I think about Megan, only she came with Laurel, and I doubt Chynna would get in the car with Laurel. And, if someone else drives us, how do we get her mother's car back? I groan. This is like some kind of demented math problem.

Chynna lurches to her feet. She sways into me, and she has to grab my shirt to keep from falling. I can smell beer on her breath, on her clothes. She smells like she's been taking a bath in beer. "I'll just have to drive myself," she says.

I put my left hand flat on her chest. She doesn't even know how to drive. With my other hand, I grab the keys. "*I'll* drive you home."

She wraps her arms around my neck. "Oh, Ben. What would I do without you?" She leans back, so she can look into my face. "You are the nicest guy in the whole world."

And the dumbest.

The pool players watch us as I sort of shove Chynna into the room and toward the stairs. As we start up, one of them says, "Get in line for a bedroom, dude." And they all laugh.

There are still kids sitting around the kitchen table. I can't tell if it's a new group. They're tossing popcorn kernels up in the air, trying to catch them in their mouths. There's a lot of popcorn on the floor.

I keep Chynna moving through into the living room. It's still crowded, but not as noisy. People are slow dancing now. Most of the lights are off. Chynna keeps tripping and stumbling. She starts to giggle, even though people are swearing at us. I look around the room, trying to spot Megan, but I don't see her.

As we pass the coffee table, Chynna grabs a half-full bottle of beer and drinks it before I can stop her.

"Chynna!"

She hands me the empty bottle, then leans toward me, looking very serious. "You don't understand, Ben," she says. "I just want to get drunk. I *need* to get drunk."

I toss the empty on the floor and shove her toward the door. "You already are drunk."

She frowns. "You could be right."

I leave her leaning against the front door while I find our jackets. It takes a while, and then it takes even longer trying to get Chynna's on her. She keeps twisting around and missing the sleeves. I finally just drape it over her shoulders.

As she stumbles out onto the porch, Kyle says, "Ben."

He's standing in the hallway leading to the bathroom. Laurel is a little ways behind him. She looks like maybe she's been crying. Kyle moves closer to me. "I'm really sorry about this, man." He nods his head toward Chynna, working her way down the steps.

I look at Chynna, then at him. I'm trying to figure out if he planned this. If he knew all along that he was going to dump all over her.

"I never thought Laurel would show up." Kyle spreads his hands. "Really, man."

I shake my head. "It's okay. I understand." And the weird thing is, I sort of do.

"You found a ride, right? I mean, you're not going home with somebody who's wasted?"

"No," I say. "We found somebody sober."

He punches my arm. "I won't forget this."

I don't think I will, either. "No problem," I say.

Outside, Chynna is bending over the door to a green Datsun. When I walk up to her, she straightens up so fast, she nearly hits me in the nose. "Omigod. Someone's painted my mom's car green." She starts to laugh, a loud, braying laugh. She has to lean against the car to keep from falling down. Joelle's jacket is gone.

"Wrong car, Chynna." I turn her around, put my hands on her shoulders, and push her toward her mom's car. She makes little chugging noises. "We're a train," she says. "I'm the engine, and you're the caboose."

We pass a blue Sentra. Patterson and Tiffani are leaning against the trunk. Patterson is looking down at his feet. Tiffani has her arm around his shoulders, her forehead against the side of his head. They don't see us.

We finally find the car. I bundle Chynna into the passenger side, and I climb into the driver's seat. "Fasten your seat belt." It takes her three tries, but she finally does it.

I fasten mine. Then I sit there, just kind of staring at the dashboard. It's not that different from our Volvo. And a car's a car. Right? I look over at Chynna. She's leaned her head back against the headrest. She has her eyes shut.

I fit the key in the ignition and turn it, carefully. The engine starts, then stops. I turn the key again, harder, and when the engine starts, I floor the accelerator. The engine roars, loud. I jerk my foot off the pedal.

Chynna's sitting upright. "Wow," she says, and she laughs.

I look up at the house, expecting to see people lining the porch rail, pointing and laughing. But no one's there. And the engine is running.

It takes me a long time to find the headlights. I find everything else: wipers, emergency flashers, turn signals, rear defroster, heater. I leave the heat on. When I turn the wipers on for the third time, Chynna reaches across and flips a switch on the steering column. Light floods the grass in front of us. "For heaven's sake," Chynna says. I think about telling her to drive, if she knows so much, but she puts her head back and closes her eyes again.

I back up. I hardly give it any gas at all. Fortunately,

Mike's Gran Torino is gone, and I have plenty of room. Out in the driveway, I realize I've been holding my breath. I let it out in a big whoosh that makes Chynna open her eyes. And then I realize that we're facing the wrong way. We're heading toward the house.

Chynna peers out the windshield. "This doesn't look right."

I look in the rearview mirror. I could back down the driveway. But it's a long way to the road. I pull back into the space. It only takes me three tries to get out into the driveway facing the road. My hands are sweating so much, I have to wipe them on my jeans.

I drive slowly to the end of the driveway. I stop and check the road. Right, left. Right again. Left again. Just to be sure. One more time. I take a deep breath and pull out onto the pavement. No police cars come roaring up behind us, sirens wailing, lights flashing. I push the speedometer up to twenty-five.

Chynna rolls her window down and sticks her head out. "I am so drunk!" she screams.

I laugh. I can't help it. Mom never does anything like this.

Chynna pulls her head back in. "We're going awfully slow. Why are we going so slow?"

"I don't want to miss the turn," I say. But I let the speedometer up to thirty.

"That party sucked," Chynna says. She slumps back in her seat. "That party sucked dead rats."

"Yeah. Well." Actually I was starting to have an okay time, there at the end.

"I can't believe Kyle did that to me. I mean, he's been so

nice to me. At school and everything. I thought tonight was going to be just so perfect."

I'm starting to think about when we get out on Pacific Highway. There'll be more cars. I'll have to drive faster. Probably there'll be cop cars. I sit up straighter in my seat, trying to look taller, trying to look sixteen.

Chynna gives a big sniff. "What a moron."

"Kyle?"

"No. Me." And all of a sudden she's crying again, just wailing.

I push down on the gas pedal, and the needle wavers up to thirty-five.

The stop sign looms suddenly out of the darkness. I have to brake a little too hard, and we screech to a stop. I look both ways up and down the road. It's really dark. "We turned left here? When we came? Didn't we?" Chynna doesn't answer. I ease my foot onto the gas and turn right.

This road is wider, and I let the speedometer go right back up to thirty-five. I flex my hands on the wheel. I'm feeling pretty good. This isn't so hard. In fact, it's easier without Mom over there continually yelling at me about stuff I already know or cars I've already seen. I glance at Chynna. She's bending over, wiping her eyes on the hem of her sweater.

A road sign flashes by. "Sherwood?" I ease my foot up off the gas. "Did that say Sherwood?"

Chynna looks around. "What? Where's Sherwood?"

The wrong friggin' way, I think. I let the car slow down more. I look in the rearview mirror, trying to see if there's a sign the other way, but it's too dark.

Chynna's hand drops onto my leg, and I jump so high I

nearly hit my head on the ceiling. She leans closer, the way she did when Kyle was driving. She tightens her hand on my leg. "You think I'm attractive and sexy, right?"

The light from the dashboard is throwing weird, black shadows across her face. Her makeup's still smeared. She looks like someone out of *Night of the Living Dead*. The remake, with the better special effects. I look back at the road. "Sure. Sure I think you're attractive."

She leans closer and her hand moves farther up and inside my leg. I want to watch it, but I have to watch the road. "And you'd like to have sex with me."

I look at her. Here? Now? And for a second, I think . . . I still have the condom. . . . And then I think about Megan. I sigh. "You know, Chynna . . ." I look back at the road. A rabbit or something furry is crouched, frozen, in the headlights. "Oh shit!" I hit the brakes hard and crank the wheel to the side.

The brakes lock. The tires screech on the wet road. I see a blur as the rabbit leaps out of the way. The back tires start to skid. Chynna is hanging onto the dashboard, her eyes big and wide. I know there's something I'm supposed to do. Turn in the direction of the skid? Turn in the opposite direction? It seems like I have a lot of time to think about it. I can't remember, so I just hang onto the wheel as we turn in a big, slow circle. And I keep hanging on as we go off the edge of the road.

# Chapter
## Sixteen

I'm afraid we're going to tip over. But there's no ditch or anything. No fence. No trees. No barn. We roll across the grassy edge and stop, hard, in an empty field.

We both just sit there. Neither one of us says anything. The headlights are shining on a big old pine tree. It's pretty far away. I sit there, trying to figure how far away it is. From the twenty-yard line to the goalpost, maybe?

Chynna lets go of the dashboard. "Holy cow," she says. "Holy cow."

I shake my head. "No cows. Thank God."

She gives me a funny look. "Are you okay?"

"Yeah. Sure. I'm fine." I open my door. "I'm going to check the car." I step out, and immediately sink my Doc Martens in mud. I stand there, taking deep breaths. When my heart finally slows down, I turn and look at the Honda. I don't know what I'm looking for. But once, when we spun out on our way up Mt. Hood, Dad got out and checked the car.

I walk around to Chynna's side. The ground here is drier and grassier. Her side looks okay, too. I squat down. The only thing I can see is that the tires are sunk in the mud. Especially the back one on the driver's side.

I go back around to my door. I try to wipe off some of the mud before I get back in. "I think it's okay," I say. "I think we can just drive out."

Chynna nods. Her lips are pressed together. I wonder if she's mad at me. Which sort of makes me mad. It's not like this was my idea. It wasn't even my fault. She was the one distracting me, talking to me. "I think I can sort of curve us back onto the road." I look at the tree. It looks closer now. More like the ten-yard line.

Chynna nods again.

I start the engine and press down on the gas. The car lurches once, and then stops moving. The engine's still running, though, and I can hear the tires spinning.

"What's wrong?" Chynna's voice is small and tight, like it barely makes it out of her mouth.

"It's sort of muddy." I give the car more gas. The back tires are whining. We're not moving at all. I give it more gas. The whining gets louder, angrier.

"It's not working," Chynna says. "Why aren't we going?"

The tires are squealing. "Because we're stuck!" I shout it, really loud. I take my foot off the gas and lean my head against the steering wheel. Godammit. "Godammit!"

"Can't you push it out or something?"

I lift my head. "I can push if you can drive."

She spreads her hands flat out in front of her. "No way. I've never driven anything. And I don't have a permit."

"You don't need a permit to drive across a field," I say, although I'm not sure that's true. I turn off the engine. "I'll go check again."

The back tire on my side is sunk past the hub cap. The one on Chynna's side is almost as bad.

I've seen TV shows where people get cars unstuck. I know we need something for traction. Rocks or boards or something. Only the field around us is empty. Even the pine tree doesn't have any branches close to the ground.

Chynna's door opens, and she gets out. She stands there, very straight and still. Her face looks really pale in the moonlight. "I think I'm going to barf," she says. She takes a few steps away from the car, bends over, and throws up.

I am totally grossed out. I walk a little ways back toward the road. Getting away from the sound and the smell. Thinking about it, I start to think I might throw up.

By the edge of the road, I find a big tuft of grass. I spend some time wiping the mud off my shoes. When they're both pretty clean, I walk back.

Chynna is leaning against the car, her head on the hood. I stop next to the trunk. "Are you okay?"

She shakes her head without lifting it up. She groans. Then she turns around and sits down, suddenly, her back sliding down the side of the car.

"Chynna!" I vaguely remember something in seventh-grade health—or was it on *True Stories of Paramedics?*—about alcohol poisoning. How much did she actually drink tonight? I kneel down beside her. "Chynna?"

She opens one eye. "Don't yell. Just please, please, don't yell." The eye closes again.

"You can't sit here on the ground. It's too cold."

"I don't care." Suddenly she gets up in a half crouch, scurries a few steps and throws up again.

I walk to the back of the car. I look at the tires. Still stuck. I look around at the tree and the field and the road. No cars. No houses. No nothing.

I'm starting to feel just a little panicky. We can't stay out here all night. She's throwing up. She might have alcohol poisoning. She might freeze to death. And I remember that I'm supposed to be taking care of her. I'm the guy. I'm supposed to know what to do.

Chynna is back by the car again, leaning against her door. She has one hand pressed over her mouth, like that's going to keep stuff in.

"I think maybe I should walk back to the party," I say. "It should only take me . . ." A few days. "A few minutes."

Chynna says something.

"What?"

She takes her hand away from her mouth. "There's a cell phone. In the glove compartment." She claps her hand back over her mouth.

A phone. In the glove compartment. I clench my fist and do a little victory dance. A phone. In the glove compartment. I go around to my side of the car and dig it out.

Only who am I going to call? I don't know where Mom is or Grandma. Chynna's parents aren't home. I don't know Todd's dad's girlfriend's number. I think about Jeremy and his parents. Jeremy's parents are pretty nice. Only I can't call them now, in the middle of a field, halfway to Sherwood.

Outside, Chynna moans.

I dig out my wallet. The scrap of paper is still there, behind my Blockbuster Video card, right where I put it back last May, when Dad gave it to me.

I sit down with the door open and my feet out in the mud. I dial the number.

It rings four times, and I'm starting to think I'm going to get a machine, when someone picks up. "Hello?"

It's not Dad. "Uh. Hi. Can I talk to . . . Steve?"

There's silence on the other end. Then the voice says, "Is this Ben?"

"Yeah. Yeah, it is."

"This is Keith."

No fooling. "Can I talk to my dad?"

"He's not here, Ben. He went to have coffee with his mom."

"Grandma? He's with Grandma?"

"Right. He left—oh, I don't know. About an hour ago. Maybe a little less. I'm not sure when he'll be back."

"They're drinking coffee in the middle of the night?"

"Well. It's ten-thirty. I guess that is kind of late." Keith sounds worse on the phone than he does in real life.

I look at the clock on the radio. It *is* only ten-thirty. It seems like this night has lasted for days. It seems like I've been out in this field for days.

"I'll tell him you called, Ben. And I know he'll be really pleased. He'll call right back."

He's going to hang up, and I don't want this calm, adult voice to go away. No matter what he sounds like. "It's just . . ." I start, and I have to stop, because I know I'm going to cry. I take a deep breath.

"Is something wrong? Can I help with something?"

I take another breath. "We're sort of stuck."

"Stuck?"

"The car. The car is stuck."

"You and your mom?"

"No. Me and Chynna. The girl . . ."

"With the belly button. I remember." *He* takes a deep breath. "Let me get this straight. You're out somewhere alone, and you've gotten the car stuck."

"In mud," I say.

"In mud." He's quiet. "Were you driving?"

"Sort of."

Another silence. He's probably getting ready to list all the reasons this is stupid. He's probably going to ask if I have a signed permission form. He's probably going to call the cops. "Sorry," he says, suddenly. "I had to find a paper and pen. Where are you, exactly?"

"In a field." My mind goes completely blank. "A big field."

"Ben." Keith sounds exasperated. He actually sounds just a little like Dad.

"No. No, wait. There's directions around here some-where." I scrabble around on the floor. As long as Kyle didn't take them with him. But they're under Chynna's seat. "We're . . . well, I guess about four or five miles on Clackamas Road. Off Pacific Highway. We're just past the turn off for Wy'east Road?"

"I think I know where that is," he says. "There's a great U-pick place out that way. Toward Sherwood, right?"

"Right." I close my eyes. "Could you . . . can you be here sort of soon?"

"I'll be there as soon as I can," he says, and he hangs up without saying good-bye.

I turn off the cell phone and put it back, carefully, in the glove compartment. I climb out of the car.

Chynna is lying flat on her back in the grass. She has her eyes clamped tight shut. "Whenever I open my eyes, everything spins around," she says.

"You're going to freeze out here." I take her hand and pull her to her feet. She stands there, swaying, and I'm afraid she's going to throw up again. On me. But she doesn't. She stumbles over to the car. I get the back door open, and she falls, face first, onto the seat. I fold her legs in after her and shut the door. I get in the front passenger seat.

"Who did you call?" Chynna asks, her voice muffled by the upholstery.

"A friend of my dad's."

I lean over and turn the key far enough to start the heater. I run it for about five minutes, but then I remember this TV show where this woman stranded in her car died of carbon monoxide poisoning. So I shut it off.

I keep watch in the rearview mirror for car lights. And I start thinking that maybe it was dumb to call Keith. I mean. What good is he going to do? It's not likely that a guy like him can help. Dad was never any good with cars. There's no way Keith is going to be able to get a car unstuck.

"I can't go back to school on Monday," Chynna says, so suddenly it makes me jump. "Everybody will know Kyle dumped me." She groans. "And I lost Joelle's jacket." She presses her face back down in the upholstery.

I think about Monday. I jam my hands in my pockets, and I find the condom. I pull it out and look at it. Then I roll down the window and toss it out.

Finally, I see lights coming slowly down the road. I click on the Honda's headlights and get out of the car.

A big Jeep Cherokee pulls up at the side of the road. My heart starts to hammer. Oh, terrific. A big old Jeep. It's going to be full of huge, scary rednecks. They'll kill me. Attack Chynna. I've seen the movie.

Only Keith jumps down from the passenger's side. He's wearing jeans and an old ski jacket and Doc Martens like mine. A younger man in jeans and a down jacket comes around from the driver's side.

"Ben," Keith says. "This is Greg. He's a friend of your dad's and mine."

"Hey, there," Greg says. He sticks out his hand, and I shake it. His hand is big and rough. He sort of reminds me of Mr. Brown, the varsity coach. Only younger. "What happened?"

"There was a rabbit in the road."

He nods, like this makes sense, and walks over to the Honda.

"Are you all right?" Keith asks. "Both of you?"

"We're fine. Chynna's in the car."

He follows Greg. I start to warn them about the mud and their shoes, but it's too late and neither of them seems to care.

They both look in the back window at Chynna. "You're sure she's okay?"

"I think so. She's kind of . . ." I hesitate.

"Drunk," Greg says. He bends down and looks under the front of the car.

Keith is looking at me. "Have you been drinking?"

"No."

I'm not sure he believes me, but he just turns to Greg. "Can you pull it out?"

Greg straightens up. "No problem." He grins at me. "I just love a chance to use my four-wheel drive and my winch."

As he's maneuvering the Jeep in front of the Honda, Chynna sits up. She gets out and walks, slowly, over to Keith and me. She has her arms wrapped tight around her. "What's going on?"

"He's pulling us out," I say.

Keith takes off his jacket and puts it on her. He's much better at it than I was.

Greg has the Honda out and on the road in about five minutes. As he's unhooking the cable from the axle, Keith says, "I think I'd better drive you guys home."

I don't say anything. I just get in the passenger seat. Chynna flops, face up this time, in back. Keith gets in the driver's seat. He glances back at Chynna. "You might want to sit up, honey. Lying down back there is just going to make it worse."

Chynna moans, but she sits up.

I direct Keith to our street. Greg follows. Keith pulls the Honda into Chynna's driveway. The house is still dark. Kyle's truck is still parked by the curb. The only thing different is Greg, idling the Jeep at the end of the driveway.

We all get out. Chynna hands Keith the jacket. "Thanks."

He looks at me, then he hands Chynna the keys. "These must be yours." He pats her arm. "Try to drink a lot of fluids, sweetie."

We watch her walk up the steps to her front door. She fumbles with the lock then goes inside.

"She is going to feel awful in the morning," Keith says.

I kick at the mud on the tire. "You gonna tell my dad?"

Keith sighs. "I probably should."

I look at him.

"But I probably won't."

I come this close to hugging him. "God. Man. Thanks. Thanks for everything."

He holds up his hand. "Just don't do it again."

"No way."

He smiles. "Well. It was nice to see you again, Ben."

"Yeah. Yeah. You, too." And I mean it.

He gets in the Jeep. Greg waves as they drive away.

I think maybe I should get a hose. Maybe try to clean some of the mud off the car. But I say, "Oh, screw it." And I go home.

# Chapter
## Seventeen

Grandma gets home around eleven-thirty. I'm watching a rerun of *The X-Files*. "Hi, Grandma."

"Hi." She sets her purse down on the counter and takes off her coat. She holds it draped over her arm. "This is the episode where they're in the woods. With the cloud of little green bugs."

I twist around to look at her. "I didn't know you watched this show."

She smiles, not a real happy smile. "I think that David Duchovny is pretty cute."

I laugh. Then I pat the couch beside me. "You want to sit down and watch?"

"No. No. I'm tired." But she comes and stands next to the arm of the couch. She strokes her coat, like it's a cat or something. "I went and saw your father tonight."

"No kidding." I keep my face blank.

"I'm thinking I need to get on home, and I just couldn't . . . well . . . he's my only son." She's still staring at the coat, like she's talking to it and not to me.

Scully screams her high-pitched scream, and we both look at the TV. "Whoa," I say. "That's sort of gross."

"Yes, it is," Grandma says, and we watch for a little bit. When the commercial comes on, Grandma says, "Have you met this Keith?"

"Yeah," I say. I look up at her. "I have met him."

She nods.

"He's a pretty nice guy," I say.

She nods again. "That's some comfort, I suppose." She doesn't sound comforted. "Not that anything makes this any easier." She frowns down at me. I can see the powder or whatever she uses stuck down in the wrinkles around her mouth. "And you're doing okay?"

"I'm doing fine, Grandma." I think about it. "Just fine," I add.

She leans over and pats me on the shoulder. "Good night, Ben."

"Good night, Grandma."

She picks up her purse and goes off down the hall. I hear her bedroom door shut. I turn the volume down on the TV. It almost looks like Mulder and Scully are both dead at the end, but they get saved in the last two minutes.

I click the TV off as the credits roll. It's really quiet in the house. I can hear the murmur of the refrigerator motor and the low rumble of Grandma snoring.

Outside, I hear a dog bark.

Schottsie!

I grab an apple out of the fruit bowl on the counter, and I run out onto the porch, flipping on the light as I go. Stupid Schottsie is standing in the middle of the driveway, behind Grandma's car, barking at something across the street.

"Hey!" I shout, and I throw the apple as hard as I can, right at him. I miss, and the apple splatters into a million juicy pieces.

Schottsie yelps, leaps up, does a perfect 180 in midair and lands running. He's through the hedge and back in his yard in two seconds flat.

I laugh. And then I see what he was barking at.

Chynna is standing next to her mailbox. She's wearing pajamas and a bathrobe and some kind of fluffy slippers. I have to look twice to make sure it's her. The cat is sitting next to her. "Hi. You locked out again?"

"No." She gives the post of the mailbox a little kick. Then she looks both ways and crosses the street. The cat comes with her. She sits down on the porch step.

I sit down beside her. Her pajamas have penguins on them. "Your parents come home?"

"Not yet. They're going to be home around one."

The cat rubs against my legs. I guess he's forgiven me. Or he doesn't know who I am. "What's his name?"

"Sparky." Chynna leans over her knees so I can't see her face. "Kyle came and got his truck."

She's right. The curb is empty.

"I heard him, and I came outside. That was so stupid. I should have just stayed in the house. I should have just . . . you know."

"Yeah," I say, although I don't know if I do know.

"Laurel drove him over. So he could jump-start his truck."

"Oh." Now I know. Sparky jumps up on my lap, spreads himself across my knees. He's furry and heavy and very warm.

"I thought . . . well . . . some of that stuff tonight, some of it I don't remember so well. Some of it, I thought, maybe I was just remembering wrong. Or, like, I wasn't understanding it exactly."

"But not about Laurel," I say.

She tilts her head back. "Turns out I got the Laurel part exactly right. I guess he really likes her."

"That sucks," I say.

"You shouldn't have to hear stuff like that in your pajamas, you know. And with her like sitting there, holding the jumper cables."

"Right."

"Plus, I feel absolutely awful." She puts her head in her hands. "I have the worst headache I've ever had in my entire life."

"I bet."

She looks at me out of the corners of her eyes. "Did I throw up a whole lot? Was it totally disgusting?"

She looks really miserable. Her eyes are still red. Her hair's all straggly, like she washed it but didn't dry it completely. She looks really young, like a sixth grader. And she's wearing pajamas with penguins on them. "It wasn't *totally* disgusting," I say.

She puts her head back down on her knees. We both just sit there for a while, not saying anything. I rub Sparky under the chin, and he starts purring. All of a sudden, Chynna says, "This is a nice porch."

It's just a cement slab. Not a fancy wooden thing, like the

one at Todd's. But I say, "Yeah. It is a nice porch." I reach out and put my hand on the cold cement. "My dad used to bring me out here when I was sick."

She lifts her head and looks at me. "What?"

I laugh, partly because of the look on her face, partly because I'm remembering. "No, see, I used to get this cough, this croup thing, when I was little. Late at night. You cough, and you can't breathe. But cold air helps. The doctor told my parents they should just take me outside. So my dad would wrap me up in a blanket, and he'd carry me out here, and I'd sit in his lap." I haven't thought about this in a long time. And, remembering it now, I can feel how the tightness in my chest would loosen up. I can feel my lungs filling with air.

Chynna is sitting up straight, looking at me. "That's nice, though. It's a nice story."

"Yeah," I say. "Yeah. It is." I rub the cat's ears, and he purrs louder. "He's gay, you know."

She frowns. "Sparky?"

I laugh. "No, you moron. My dad. Him and Keith. They live together. They're both gay."

The look on her face is great. "Your dad? The big guy? The football guy?"

"Yeah. That's the one. Sexual preferences other than the norm. Homosexual. Queer. Fairy . . ."

"I get the picture, Ben." Chynna's still frowning at me. "Was he always . . . ?"

"I guess so. He just told us last May. My mom and me."

"Holy cow," Chynna says, and she sounds just like she did back when the car went off the road. "That must have been quite a moment."

Back in May, he said, "Someday, Ben, I hope you'll think about forgiving me." I lift Sparky up, so his head is right under my chin. "It was quite a moment, all right."

"And now he lives with this Keith guy?"

"Yep." Sparky squirms, gives a little yowl, and I put him down gently on the cement between us.

Chynna's shaking her head. "That really, really sucks, Ben."

I think about Keith showing up with Greg and the Jeep, showing up as fast as he could. I think about him saying he won't tell Dad. "It could be worse," I say, finally.

Chynna gives a little shudder. Then she turns toward me. She looks serious, like she's going to tell me something very important. "You know what?"

"What?"

"My name's not really Chynna."

No, duh. "It's not?" I say.

"Uh-uh. It's really Gail."

"No kidding."

She nods. "It is. Gail Mapes." She makes a face. "Jeez. What a stupid name."

Sparky has folded himself up into a neat package, his feet and tail all tucked in underneath him. "What made you change your name?"

She shrugs. "I dunno. We moved here, and my dad made this big deal about how this was a fresh start for all of us, how we were going to start all over again. And I thought, well, okay. Nobody knows me at this school. I don't have to be boring old Gail Mapes anymore. I can be whoever I want to be."

"And you wanted to be . . . ?" Weird, I'm thinking.

"Popular," she says. She leans forward and wraps her arms around her knees. "And mysterious. And . . . I don't know . . . just more interesting."

It sounds like a lot to be, all at one time. But I nod. "I guess you did that."

She grins. "It was sort of fun, actually. You can tell people just about anything."

"Like that you made it with a guy in the band room?"

She sighs. "That wasn't so good. Joelle was bugging me, and I just sort of said the first thing I thought of. Later, you know, I thought I should have said, like, a jock. A lacrosse player, maybe. That would be sort of different."

It would be really different at Willamette View. We don't even have a lacrosse team. "How about getting stoned in the bathroom? And setting it on fire?"

"Now that one was pretty good, I thought." She looks up at me. "You wouldn't believe the stuff people will fall for. I told this one girl in my science class that I'm a Satanist, and she made the teacher move her to another desk."

We both laugh.

"Are you?" I ask, after a second.

"What?"

"A Satanist?"

"No. Of course not."

I look out at the empty street. I try to keep my voice level. "Ever been stoned?"

"No."

"Ever had sex?"

I know she looks at me again, that quick, sideways, look.

"No." She looks back out at the street. "How about you?"

Actually, I'm really sort of flattered that she asks. "No," I say.

We're both quiet. Sparky stretches, opens his mouth wide in a big, ugly cat yawn, and walks off to sit under Grandma's car. I think about Kyle pretending to be a stud. And Jeremy pretending to be Christian. And Amber Parks pretending to be such a perfect suck-up.

Chynna sits forward, her arms wrapped around her knees. "That Megan girl asked about you."

"When?"

"Tonight. She was in Laurel's car. She asked if I knew where you'd gone. I said, home. And then she asked where you live."

"What did you say?"

"I said you live across the street." She grins. "And I said we were just friends."

"Great," I say.

She stands up and stretches her arms above her head. Her bathrobe has come open, and her pajama top rises up. I can see the ring in her belly button. "I gotta go. I want to be in bed before my parents get home."

"What are you going to tell them about the car? It's pretty muddy still."

She shrugs. "I'll tell them Kyle's car wouldn't start and we had to take that car to the party." She shrugs again. "Which is absolutely true."

I nod. "Yeah. It is."

"Is your dad's . . . friend going to tell anybody, you think?"

"I don't think so."

She nods. "That's very understanding of him. But, guys like that are supposed to be more sensitive."

"Yeah. Some of them are, I guess."

"Yeah." She puts her slippered foot on the step beside me. "I won't tell anybody at school about your dad."

I'm not sure that it matters. Right now, it doesn't seem to have a lot to do with me. But it might. It might matter more on Monday. "Thanks," I say.

She slides her foot up and down. Finally she gives me a little kick on the knee. "And you don't tell anybody about my name. Okay?"

"You're still going to be Chynna?"

"Of course. Why wouldn't I be?"

I shrug.

"Although I am thinking about, you know, maybe no more football players for a while."

"Football's over now, anyway," I say. I mean it as a joke, but she doesn't laugh.

She sighs. "Kyle was such a jerk."

Or maybe he was just pretending to be a jerk, too.

"I was thinking maybe I'd sort of take a break," Chynna says. "You know. Look around. Check things out. Not commit."

"Save yourself," I say. No more bodyguards.

She looks at me. Then she grins. "Exactly."

I grin back. "Sounds like a good idea."

She kicks my knee again. "See you Monday, then." And she crosses the street to her house.

I think about sitting there on the porch until Mom gets

home. But my butt is turning to solid ice. I get up and go inside and turn the TV back on. I flip through the channels. *Alien* is on HBO. I sit back, and I watch it all the way to the end. And she does look great in her underwear. I think about calling Dad and telling him. But I decide to wait until tomorrow.